COLLEEN

Erin Louis

A HellBound Books LLC Publication
Copyright © 2023 by HellBound Books Publishing
LLC
All Rights Reserved

Cover and art design by Tee Art for
HellBound Books Publishing LLC

No part of this book may be reproduced, stored in a
retrieval system, or transmitted by any means, electronic,
mechanical, photocopying, recording or otherwise without
written permission from the author
This book is a work of fiction. Names, characters, places
and incidents are entirely fictitious or are used fictitiously and
any resemblance to actual persons, living or dead, events or
locales is purely coincidental.

www.hellboundbookspublishing.com

Printed in the United States of America

COLLEEN

1

I hate funerals. I guess it would be weird if I liked them, but I wouldn't be the least bit shocked if it were someone's kink. I heard of a guy once whose kink was getting kicked in the balls. Viewed in that light, a funeral kink doesn't seem so weird. It isn't however... my kink. And my neighbor's funeral sucked more than most. But Colleen insisted that we attend. Of course, it was much easier for her. She didn't have to concern herself with how she looked to the other mourners.

I say other mourners, as if I was in mourning too. I was not really. I didn't dislike Mary, but I couldn't say that I was going to miss her either. That sounds mean, but Colleen assured me that Mary is in a better place. And Colleen should know, she's dead too. So really, I should be happy for her. Hopefully Mary's better place is better than a dusty old church. Any place that doesn't smell like Pine Sol and unrepentant mildew would be a better place in my humble opinion.

It may have been her idea to come, but that didn't make it any easier on me. I had to keep my eyes focused on the guy speaking at the podium. He had been crying, and not in a manly way. But a in wet, phlegmy, ugly way. Which is probably fair considering that Mary was his mother. And he was going to miss her. Although, had he been around more, she might still be alive. She was all alone in her house after all. I would have loved to have been able to tell him that, but Colleen said it that would be a bad idea. Colleen was always right. Well, mostly always.

Colleen has had a few bad ideas. Dropping the cherry bomb in the toilet of my last job being one of the worst. I was going to quit anyway, and God knows the manager deserved it. I don't think I'm cut out for restaurant work anyway. But the misdemeanor on my record and the subsequent fine hadn't been worth it at all. It made getting another job much harder. I wasn't sure how I would find another, but Colleen assured me something would come up.

The guy finally finished speaking and the priest or pastor or whatever started talking again. I'm not even sure what flavor of church it was. Religion has never been my thing. In fact, I assumed, wrongly I know now, that there wasn't anything other than what was here on earth. But once Colleen showed up, I had to admit that there was at least something else out there. It's one thing to see a ghost. It's a whole other thing to have one as your best friend.

"Ugh, that bloody dead guy on the cross is grossing me out. How do these people not see how twisted that is? I mean come on, so God had sex with a teenager to have his son. Then has him killed to make up for the bad things the people he created did? It makes a great horror story, but man it's pretty sick when you think about it."

Had she been solid, I would have jabbed her with my elbow to shut her up. But Colleen didn't make herself visible in public for obvious reasons. I turned my head and gave her my best shut up death stare. Not only did it *not* shut her up, but the lady in the next pew thought it was meant for her. She returned my death stare in kind. And dare I say she was better at it than me. Under her gray nearly purple hair, her frown almost turned me to stone. I gave her a sheepish *I'm sorry* look that I hoped would end this awkward stare stand-off. But then she flipped me the bird. I glanced around the room to see if anyone had seen the highly inappropriate and totally unwarranted gesture, but it seemed like our unintentional unspoken spat had gone unnoticed. And since no one *was* looking, I saluted her with my own middle finger.

Colleen, totally unfazed kept going, "I mean did she even consent? What was she like thirteen? He couldn't find someone a bit older? God must be a pervert or something. Not to mention the whole blood sacrifice thing. Couldn't he just have made people not sin? He's supposed to be omnificent, isn't he? He could do anything, but decided executing his own son was the way to go. He seems like a real asshole, I…"

"Dude, I get it, God is a dick."

The old guy in the pew in front of me turned around and looked at me like I was Satan herself, then put a finger to his lips and hushed me. My cheeks turned red, totally clashing with the turquoise streaks in my black hair. Colleen was giggling, and I decided it was time to go before I caught her giggles and really looked like a lunatic. Laughing alone at my elderly neighbor's funeral would not have been a good look.

I got up and crept out of the church. Pretending not to notice the other people staring at me as I walked out the door. The sunlight hit me like a yellow freight train. One I wasn't at all prepared for. Although, how *does* one prepare to get hit by a freight train? I squinted and blinked my eyes until I could see again. The fresh air I took into my lungs made up for the sun's assault on my eyeballs. I felt the relief from being out of the church trickle down from the top of my head to my combat boots.

"It's way better out here. It smelled like old people farts in there," Colleen said.

"You don't even have a real nose, and it's been like a thousand years since you've smelled a fart."

"That's not nice. I'm not that old. And I can smell stuff when I want to. No reason to be mean Lacey. Let's go home and binge Netflix and eat pizza naked."

Colleen had to go solid to eat pizza. It's not my favorite really, but it is fun to watch her stuff a whole piece in her mouth. And she loved ham and pineapple pizza, which was the only kind I really liked.

"And then you can smell *my* farts."

"You don't fart, and stop being so gross." I tried to be serious but couldn't stop myself from laughing as I pushed the unlock button on my car's key fob.

"Ahhh….you say that, but you're laughing. See I'm helping. You were getting all bummed out about that dead old lady."

I scrunched my eyebrows together in an attempt to show her I thought she was wrong. But to no avail, because she was right. I got in and started the engine. Colleen just oozed through the closed passenger door. It would have been really weird to open the door for someone no one else could see. And I'm pretty sure I already looked like a weirdo. Although partly by design.

Richard was waiting for me when I opened the door to my little old house. He meowed at me and hissed at Colleen.

"Hey Dick! What's shaking?"

"Don't call him that, his name is Richard. And he's a good kitty. Don't be jealous."

"Pffft… jealous? Of that bag of fur? No way."

But she was jealous. Of anyone or anything that gave me attention. It's why I don't have a boyfriend. I put my foot down with Richard though. When I saw him outside my house next to the trash can, I fell in love. He was so small. His mother was nowhere in sight, and he wasn't in great shape. Dirty and starving, I took him in and washed and bottle fed him. Naming him Richard was Colleen's idea. She said he just looked like a *Richard*. I, of course, listened to her. It's too late to change it now that he knows his name. She says all cats are dicks. And once again, she's not entirely wrong.

I took off my funeral clothes and didn't bother to put any other ones on. The whole thing with Mary left a bad taste in my mouth and I was ready to forget about it. Zoning out on the TV and gorging on pizza was just the thing. And Colleen was obviously looking to get a little frisky. She was naked too, and I could no longer see the room through her ethereal form.

I didn't think I was into chicks. But kind of like pizza, when I found one that I liked I could be well…open minded. I placed an online order and before I could put my phone down, Colleen was on top of me. Her body was cold. Maybe not cold but cool to the touch. She was never completely warm. But her cool wet tongue worked just fine. Her body was what one might expect from someone not totally human anymore. She had never been clear if the way she looked now was how she looked in life. Her strawberry blond hair hung to the middle of her back, and her small, upturned nose was dotted with tiny freckles. A sexy constellation under her pale violet almost pink eyes. The rest of her was built like a porn star. Her boobs alone would be enough to convert even the most gnostic of atheists. There is something just a little off about her appearance when she chooses to come into the flesh. Hard to say exactly what it is though, just not quite human. A consequence of being a ghost and not quite human anymore, I guess.

We finished just in time to hear the knock at door. Catching my breath and standing up on wobbly legs, I grabbed my robe and staggered out to get my pizza.

"Invite him in if he's cute," Colleen called from the bedroom.

I opened the door, and he was not cute. Not ugly, but I wasn't tempted to invite him in. I paid, then shut and locked the door. I set the pizza down on the coffee table while Colleen picked up the remote to look for something to watch. The sun was setting, and I tried to forget about the events of the day. But Mary and her death was still bugging me.

"I feel kind of bad for her family."

"You worry wart," it came out like "Wawwweee waattt" because she was trying to talk around an entire slice of ham and pineapple pizza. She chewed loudly and swallowed, "She was old. And if anything, her family should be grateful. The old bag *was* suffering. Trust me, she and her family are much happier now."

"*Was* she suffering though? She was still taking herself to bible study and her knitting class every week."

"Of course, she was suffering. No one wants to live past eighty, trust me. The poor thing was eating Metamucil like candy. And now she's in heaven pooping like a spring chicken."

"Yeah, but did we have to burn her house down?"

"Well not technically, but that was an act of kindness, wasn't it? The family won't have to dig through and get rid of all her crap. Who knows? Maybe they'll get a discount on the cremation services? Plus, it was fun. Right? That old house was an eyesore anyway. OOOHHH look, a horror movie. Let's watch it!"

Colleen clicked the button to start the movie and stuffed another piece of pizza into her mouth. I picked up a piece of pizza and took a small bite, it wasn't bad. The movie wasn't either and soon thoughts of Mary drifted away.

2

I was never what you might call popular. Pretty far from it actually. I got good grades in school and learned quickly. Reading and writing were my best subjects, math was a struggle, but I managed. People were a bigger struggle. Interacting with people was a skill I hadn't ever gotten around to mastering. Could be because I always had my face stuffed in the pages of a book. Mostly the scary ones.

It was clear that I wasn't going to fit in from the time I entered kindergarten. I talked too much, and about stuff that I guess that other people thought was weird. I tried to play with the other kids. But most of the time I would get into a game or something and look up to find that I was all alone. One time I spent close to three hours hiding in a storage closet at school. When my third-grade teacher finally found me, she told me that they had called the police, thinking I had run away. I told her that I had been playing hide and seek at recess with the other kids. It turned out that after I was hidden, they all went off and played something else. I took the hint and stopped trying to play with them.

Not long after that, I found refuge in the school library. I found my friends in books. And after I worked my way through the kiddie mysteries, like *Nancy Drew* and *Goosebumps*, I moved on to the harder stuff. I wasn't allowed in the big kid section, so I had to sneak in there when the librarian wasn't looking. I would stuff them in my backpack without checking them out, then smuggle them back in when I was done. That was when I really got hooked on the morbid and macabre. My first crush was Stephen King. *IT* was my first. *Christine*, my favorite. I expanded from there, zombies, ghosts, serial killers. The more my tastes darkened, my look did too. I embraced heavy metal, music as scary as the books I liked. And I discovered that matching my look to my tastes scared the bullies away. Black from head to toe didn't make me fit in, but there was protection in deliberately fitting out. The kids in Junior high didn't pretend to play hide and seek to get me to go away. They threw insults, juvenile comments, and sometimes harder stuff, like rocks. I learned to ignore them and got by okay. The worst of the bullies ended up going away on their own.

It was just my mom and me in a small town in the northern mountains of California. My dad passed away in a head on collision when I was just a baby. She told me about him. She said he was smart and handsome. I couldn't say if he was smart or not, but handsome he was not. But I guess I can't blame her for buttering up his memory. I know she loved him, and she said he loved me. I believed that part. She never remarried but went on dates occasionally. I never met even one of her boyfriends. She was a good mom. Until she passed too. Like my dad, in a car accident just after my twentieth birthday. She didn't have much, but she left me the house free and clear.

Orphaned by drunk drivers, I've never been tempted to touch a drop of booze. Not even a taste. Maybe one day

I will, but I haven't yet. After I lost my mom, and with no real friends to speak of, I went to a really dark place. An occult shop lit by only candlelight. I'm not sure what I was looking for. I can't say I really believed in any of that stuff. Mom was an agnostic. And the only reason she was on the fence at all was because she hoped to see my dad again. She told me one time that she didn't think there was anything out there, but she just hoped there was. So maybe I had that hope too. Either way, I left that dark and dingy shop that was filled with overpriced crystals, herbs and incense with a brand-new Ouija board.

I felt kind of stupid when I unwrapped the damned thing. It's sold as a board game and that's it. I had even read some stuff about how the thing "worked". Micro muscle movements and all that, not to mention most of the time people have already worked themselves up to be freaked out. It really isn't all that complicated. People like to be scared by stuff they don't quite understand. So why did I buy the thing, I still couldn't tell you. Boredom maybe, loneliness, grief? Any way I look at it now, it solved all of those problems, but I'm not sure I would recommend it. I think I just got lucky. I wondered if I could have ended up conjuring something really awful, rather than a see-through best friend.

I don't like to half ass anything. Not even a lone session with a Ouija board. I broke out some candles. Put on some Slayer to play softly in the background I sat down cross-legged in my living room. The whole house was still furnished with the stuff I grew up with. I know what you're thinking, I was hoping to contact my parents. Maybe…maybe not. But I took a long deep breath and set my fingers down on the planchette. It didn't move.

Thinking I needed to ask some questions, I asked if anyone was there. But still nothing. I sat there for an entire hour, wishing I had spent the money on a bag of weed instead. I said I didn't *drink*. Finally, I put it away, and went to bed. I wasn't asleep long, before I woke up startled. I sat up and looked around, but there was nothing there. I had no pets, and mom had only been gone a few months, but I had always been comfortable alone. I reached under my bed to grab the baseball bat I kept under there, intending to wield it valiantly around my house in case there was an intruder. Mostly I was just playing out the fantasy of being the hero in my own story. But as I lifted it up and out, I felt an odd breeze. A cold blast of air blew my hair back. And then I saw her.

I hopped out of bed with my slugger held tight. I swung it at the figure before I realized that I could see my bedroom curtains through her form. I put all of my weight into the swing. When it simply sliced through my would-be attacker, the momentum spun me a hundred and eighty degrees and knocked me off balance. I landed hard on my ass; my jaw clanked shut painfully. The apparition just laughed.

And laughed, and laughed.

Maybe I should have been scared, but there was something about a laughing ghost, not to mention a really pretty one that just isn't that scary. I got up and turned on the light, which made her appear even more transparent. Then she spoke.

"I'm Colleen, your fairy God Ghost. I hope you didn't break your ass swinging a bat at phantom."

"Really, you couldn't come up with something better than that? You'd think with access to the spirit realm or whatever, you'd be a little cleverer."

That was three years ago, and she's been with me ever since.

Colleen has always been a little…well a lot elusive about her origins. She said her death was tragic and she didn't want to talk about it. It seemed like a dick move to keep asking, so I didn't. I asked all sorts of other questions, and she answered most of them with a joke. Sometimes funny, but mostly she just said she didn't know. I suppose being dead doesn't give someone as many answers as one might expect, but I suspected she just didn't want to tell me.

She said she was in her twenties when she died, sometime in the eighties. Although, it would have been pretty easy to guess *when* she was from. Her ripped jeans and Iron Maiden T-shirt kind of gave it away. Her outfit was old enough to be in again. Her hair was feathered in front, but she must have died before the big hair came into style. She told me that she had been chilling in the afterlife, light again on the specifics, and felt a weird pull. Like kind of sucking feeling. She fought it for a while, but finally gave in and then she was in my room. She sounded as surprised as I was to be here.

We talked all night that first night in my room. She said she didn't know how to get back, but I don't remember her trying all that hard. We just seemed to be kindred spirits. She said where she came from was boring and a little lonely. Although, once again she was vague on the details. She didn't say it outright, but I felt rude prying. I still wonder why I wasn't scared, I guess I was just that lonely. This friend, this funny, pretty sort of person just showed up. And I didn't want her to leave. So that's why I didn't ask more questions. Besides, pissing off a ghost seemed like a bad move.

Life with Colleen has been...interesting. She has a lust for life that I suppose only comes after one has been through death. It was a lust I had lost, or maybe I never had to begin with. And then there's the regular lust of course. My love life wasn't much of a life either. But she had a knack for finding Mr. Right. Mr. Right now at least, she didn't help at all with finding a Mr. Long term. A quick fling here and there, but once he looked like he was getting too comfortable, he was gone never to be heard from again. But that is probably for the best anyway, how the hell do you explain to a potential life partner that your best pal is a ghost? You don't.

And Colleen and I had our own thing. I wouldn't say I am bisexual. I mean, it's not like I'm doing it with a real live female. It's like supernatural masturbation. And hey, nothing wrong with feeling good.

While she didn't talk about her death, she didn't talk much about her life either. Even after all this time, most of the details about her life and afterlife are a mystery. She says the stuff humans come up with about good and evil and what happens after we die are all guesses based on nothing. But that's about all she's told me. I always hoped she would explain more, but I got the sense that she was keeping me in the dark for my own good.

I wish I could say that I was surprised when she suggested burning Mary's house after we discovered she was dead. But I wasn't really. It didn't seem messed up at the time. In fact, it made perfect sense. I never second guess things in the moment with Colleen. That usually comes later. At the time it just seemed like a fun thing to do. Now it does seem a little messed up. Colleen said that the lady really was better off, she was so old after all. And Colleen herself was proof that people moved on from this life. Colleen isn't bad…just mischievous. Well maybe just a little bad, but in a good way.

I also wish I could say I felt bad about sneaking into the old place that night. But I don't really. Once I lost my job, things had gotten a little rough money wise. And well, Colleen was right about Mary keeping all that cash in the shoebox in her coat closet next to a bunch of Nazi stuff. So, Mary wasn't just an innocent old lady. Colleen sometimes has these hunches about things, and advantage to being dead I suppose. I really never thought it was our fault that the old lady happened to die in her sleep on that night in particular. But it all worked out. I got some money to tide me over, and Mary's family wouldn't have the burden of dealing with all her stuff. All they have to do is cash the insurance check from the house. A win-win Colleen said.

3

A cold draft brought me up from a lovely dream I had been having. My stubborn brain tried to incorporate the uncomfortable chill into my dream in the form of an open window. But when the chill whispered in my ear, I had no choice but to open my eyes.

"The coffee is ready sleepyhead," she said.

Colleen was spooning me from behind, her delicate arm wrapped around my waist. Goosebumps prickled on my arms, but I didn't want to move. I pulled the thick fleece blankets up to compensate. Coffee sounded marvelous, but I wasn't quite ready. I have acquired enough comforters and blankets to live in an igloo. And despite Colleen's coldness, I was warm. Richard did his part by refusing to sleep anywhere other than on top of me. My little heater. He wouldn't move until I picked him up and moved him.

"I think I found a job for you."

I snuggled up against her and further down under my blankets. But Colleen's body dematerialized and leaked out of bed. Instantly I was *too* warm. I wiggled my arms out from my cocoon and gently dislodged Richard from hip where he had been precariously sleeping. He let out a tiny meow in protest. I sat up and folded down the top layer of blankets. I stretched and yawned and watched as Colleen, whole again, walked back in with two steaming mugs of hot coffee. Hers as black as night, my own mug filled with cream, sugar, and a splash of coffee.

"Seriously, I think I found the perfect thing. You can be your own boss, dress sexy, flirt with guys, and get paid in cash."

"Let me guess, bartender? That's about the last thing I want to do."

"No goofball. I know better than that," her frown made her look wounded.

"I don't want to be a hooker either."

Her frown evaporated and she started to laugh.

"Oh, come on, how fun would that be?"

I rolled my eyes. I rolled my eyes a lot around Colleen.

"But for real, hear me out."

I sipped my cream and sugar and braced myself.

"'Embers' has an open audition tonight. I know you would be awesome at it, and you can work at night, and whenever you want. It will be fun!"

"I do like cash, but that place is kind of sleazy. Plus, I can't dance to save my life."

She wore a crooked smile, that told me I wasn't going to say no.

"Pffft… you don't have to be able to dance to be a stripper."

I didn't doubt that she was right about that. I've never been to a strip club, but I didn't think those girls studied dance at Julliard.

"Well fuck it. Let's give it a try. You only live once, right?"

Colleen snort laughed and slugged me in the shoulder spilling our coffee into the pile of blankets on my bed and earning a dirty look from Richard. The irritated kitty hopped down and skulked to the kitchen where his food dish was. He'd be right back when he saw that it was empty.

Covered in coffee, I finally got out of bed. I pulled off the coffee-soaked blankets and tossed them into the washer. I filled Richard's dish and opened my cabinets. Other than an ancient container of oatmeal and a lone can of chicken soup, there wasn't much. I tried the fridge and was greeted by a half-eaten jar of marmalade and a crusty take-out box of old chow mein. I settled for a brown speckled banana from the otherwise empty bowl on the counter.

"Ok. Let's check it out. But I'll need something to wear, and we need to get some food."

I showered and dressed while Colleen watched videos on my laptop. She was obsessed with conspiracy videos. The more outlandish the better. When I walked into the living room, she was watching something about lizard people secretly taking the place of prominent politicians and celebrities.

"Hey, did you know that Penn and Teller are really space lizards? All their tricks are real, they just pretend that they're illusions. That's why they are so damned good. They are getting ready to take over the world. Selling real magic as bullshit." The guy she was watching on the screen had a face like a wrinkled tomato, and he was screaming into the camera. He looked like he was either trying to pass a kidney stone or having a heart attack.

"Meh…everybody knows that. Let's go."

I put my sunglasses on before I opened the door to the early afternoon sun. I can't say that I had ever given any real thought to being a stripper. But Colleen had a point, I hate getting up early, really hate having a boss, and Mary's shoebox cash was running out. I thought it could work out if I gave it half a try.

The corpse of Mary's house sat across the street. A slight pang of guilt tickled my belly as I got into my car. I could still smell the smoke; it had burned for some time before the firemen could put it out. Only a few charred beams and the chimney remained. I looked forward to whatever they would put in its place. It hadn't been well kept and made the rest of the street look worse than it was. The pang stung me one more time as I started to pull out of my driveway.

I drove to a nearby sex shop that I thought might have some stuff I could use. The mannequins in the window were adorned in sequins and lace and had comically large boobs. My own boobs aren't as comical, but I was confident they would do the trick anyway. A bell tinkled as I opened the door. Colleen seeped in behind me.

Colleen went straight to the back of the store that held a large display of sex toys. I was immediately grateful that no one else could see her. She was pointing to the largest purple dildo I've ever seen. Maybe the largest one in all of existence. She picked it up and began jiggling it up and down. Alarmed, I scanned the rest of the store for other people. Which was pointless really. If anyone was watching the enormous grape colored phallus doing a jig in midair, I wouldn't have to look for them, their screams would let me know they were there.

"Dude, put that down," I said as quietly as I could. Although I couldn't help but laugh. The thing was at least three feet long.

"Let's get it." She put it back on the display, where it trembled a little before lying still.

"That thing could puncture a lung. I'm good. Help me find something to wear. I'm going to need shoes too."

I headed to the clothing, if you could call it clothing, section. Costumes might be more accurate. I picked out a black thong bikini and a bra and panty set and nearly jumped out of my skin when the store attendant snuck up behind me.

"I bet those would look great on you. Would you like to try them on?" She asked. She had a voice like a cartoon character and a smile like an alligator. Her blond hair was teased into a beehive-esq type do on the top of her head.

I let her lead me to a small dressing room. Colleen squeezed in with me, unnoticed. I tried on both outfits and decided on the bikini. Simple, easy to get on and off and my favorite color. The cut flattered my modest boobs, Colleen nodded in approval.

I left the panty set on the rack outside the dressing room and headed to the wall that held some painful looking high heels. I picked out a pair of black platform high heels and asked the cartoon lady if I could try on my size. I was skeptical that I would be able to walk, let alone dance in them. And so was completely surprised when I found that they were really stable. I pranced around while Colleen made a rhythmic *oonce oonce* sound that was supposed to sound like techno dance music but sounded more like Richard coughing up a hairball.

"Welp. I think this will work." I said to Colleen who was standing to my right.

The store lady who was standing to my left looked at me funny as she led me to the counter to ring me up.

We stopped by a grocery store on the way home. Colleen watched as I lugged all the stuff into the house. We didn't have long before it would be time to go to the club. I nuked a frozen meal, slapped on some make-up and we headed out into the night.

4

Colleen

I'm not a ghost. But before you call me a liar, roll with me a moment. I am from a supernatural realm not of this earth. At least I think I am. Although, if humans ever prove it to be real, it will just be natural realm, and not super at all. I don't remember anything before I came to be with Lacey. But I don't think I was ever human. I am from what I can tell, what some refer to as a succubus. A sex demon if you will. Much harder to explain to a human than a ghost. Lacey might not have taken to me as she had if I told her that. So, I fudged just a little. Not quite a ghost, and not quite a liar.

I didn't need the Ouija board to come through, I was doing that before. In fact, I'm pretty sure Ouija boards are complete bullshit. Absolutely zero danger of summoning anything other than a self-induced case of the heebie jeebies. If a demon or ghost wants to find you, they'll do it all on their own, I think. But it made a convenient excuse to finally introduce myself. When I first came to Lacey in her school library, I hadn't intended on contacting her. At least not then. She was a child. I'm a demon not an asshole.

Well sometimes I'm an asshole, but that really all depends on your definition of asshole. But I digress.

Lacey kind of breezes over the bully thing. She makes it out like it was no big deal. But those damned kids were ruthless. Awful little turds they were. When I found Lacey, she was lonely and scared most of the time. I was with her the whole time. Watching, maybe influencing her just a little. I can be just a little manipulative I suppose, but I am a demon after all. And my heart, if I have one, is always in the right place. Well, mostly.

But I was watching out for her. When her main nemesis, Vivian, a tall blond and very popular girl came down with a wicked case of herpes, that was me. Or at least I think it was. Before you get all judgy again, let me tell you, she deserved it. She got up every morning to make Lacey's life as miserable as she could. With her flawless skin and legions of middle school minions, she needed to be knocked off her pedestal. And properly humbled, she finally left my poor Lacey alone. If you think about it, I saved that bully's life. She learned an ugly lesson about about being ugly and eventually stopped her snotty ways. At least she did until she was hit by that bus. Not me, I swear. Well, it could have been just a little me.

I didn't intend to fall in love with Lacey. And as a succubus, I'm really not supposed to. But from what I can tell it happens from time to time. And is that really so bad? Love is good, right? She's not lonely anymore, and we have a blast together.

Maybe one day I'll tell her about the demon thing, but she doesn't really need to know that right now. Not to mention, I'm not entirely sure that's what I am anyway. She is so curious about the afterlife, and I am still not sure what to tell her. The truth is, I swear it's the truth, is that I don't know much about it all myself. Sure, I might be a demon and from another realm, but I'm in the dark about my existence as much as humans are. I think there could be a god and a devil, but I've never met either. Although from what I've learned on earth, God doesn't seem like the good guy. I chose the eighties rocker look, because I knew she liked metal and as a ghost she wouldn't expect me to look modern.

And yeah, I can confidently say that Mary is in a better place. I couldn't tell you if that is heaven or not. I have no clue if heaven exists, but I can tell you that house was a real dump. I didn't mean to kill her either. It kind of happened by accident. A few times while Lacey was sleeping, I crept into the old lady's house. Really, I was just curious, and happened to find the shoebox full of cash in her closet. But next to it I also found some old Nazi paraphernalia. Nice well-meaning old people don't keep that kind of stuff. Is stealing from a Nazi really that bad? My conscience was clear.

But I really didn't mean to kill her, I just wanted to scare her a little. Give her a nightmare and make sure she stayed asleep. That's it. But I am a very specific kind of demon, a sex demon. So, what was meant to just be a bad night of sleep, turned into a kind of fatal wet dream. My bad for sure, but still not intentional. At least she went out with a bang. Orgasms were probably well in her past at that point. So really, I did her a favor. See I'm a good demon. Burning the house down, well maybe that was kind of shitty. But when I saw that Lacey had forgotten gloves and the amount of cash she had found, it was necessary. Her family might notice it was missing, and I'm not here to get Lacey in trouble. At least not serious trouble, so we burnt it down. But in the end, it all worked out for the best. Her family doesn't have to deal with all her stuff, they get an insurance check for the house, and Lacey got some cash to tide her over. Cash she is now using to start her new job. I'm a good helper.

I have no doubt that she'll kill it tonight. I'll make sure of it actually. She looks damned cute in that little bikini.

5

Why I was surprised when I walked into Embers, I have no idea. It smelled like an ashtray that someone had puked in, then spritzed with cheap perfume. My shoes seemed to stick to the floor. The lady at the door had a sour look on her face. It could have been the odor, but I think it was just her face.

"Twenty dollars," she half growled. She tilted her head towards her tip jar while deadpanning me, "Plus tip if you want a decent seat."

"Uh, I'm here for the contest."

She looked at me with thinly veiled disgust, "Mmmmm….."

She wasn't doing much for my confidence, but that seemed to be on purpose. She had the look of someone who had been sitting in that seat at the door for decades, making as many people as miserable as possible. At one point, she must have been very pretty, but her aggressive frown lines had metastasized into an unflattering roadmap of unhappiness on her face. Her red hair and dark make-up were impeccable, which made me think that she might have been a dancer once.

"Wow," I looked at the moldering name tag she wore, "Angel… your hair is just beautiful," I said as fake sincerely as I could while I dropped a five-dollar bill in her jar hoping I could win some sort of courtesy. Her face didn't budge. If that was Botox, she had too much.

Her tone lightened slightly as she said, "Go over there to the bar and talk to Rick the manager, he's the bald guy in the suit.

I smiled as I walked away, the door lady lifted the corner of her mouth in a sneer that was probably as close to a smile as she could muster.

"Break a leg."

I smiled a real smile back at her, although I'm pretty sure that she really wanted me to break a leg.

Colleen was a cool draft behind me, gently blowing me toward the bar and the guy who was obviously Rick the manager. He looked at me as I approached.

"Hi, I'm here for the contest, my name is...Lacey."

"Is it? That sucks, that would make a great stripper name." He looked at me up and down as if I were a show pony. "You're hired." He smiled what appeared to be a genuine smile, but after dealing with Angel, I had my doubts.

"Oooooo... how about Lilith?" Colleen cooed in my ear.

"You don't want me to audition?"

"Nope, it's a Tuesday night, we're short on girls and you look like you have nice tits. Unless you're hiding some wicked burn scars or something. The contest is canceled tonight. We don't have enough girls."

"Um ok." I was starting to freak out a little bit, what the hell had Colleen gotten me into?

Seeming to read my mind she said, "You're going to do great. Trust me I know."

Trust me, I know usually preceded some first class fuckery on her part, but I really didn't have much to lose.

If he hadn't been introduced to me as a strip club manager, I might have guessed he was a used car salesman. He wasn't technically bald, as there were a few stray hairs clinging stubbornly to the top of his shining dome. He looked to be in his late fifties, with a large build that strained his suit coat. Could've been a former body builder maybe. So far everyone I had met looked like they were past their prime and resentful of it.

"Angel!" He called, "Take what's her name to the dressing room and show her around."

Angel said nothing as she peeled her considerable butt off the tiny stool. The stool looked relieved to have her gone. Not because of her size, but because she reeked of unpleasantness. She walked past me, and I followed her deeper into the club. The miserable essence that engulfed her dissipated as she smiled at Rick, giving me a glimpse of her former beauty. The sticky sweet smile she gave him was returned by the manager in kind.

The rest of the club didn't actually look that bad. There were a few dozen decent looking men, sitting on the couches that lined the walls, and at the tables strewn about the large room. A big disco ball that hung from the ceiling tossed colored lights on the ceiling and walls. They were all watching the girl on stage dance to an R&B song I hadn't heard of. She was tall, thin with skin the color of light coffee, with a cute butt and small breasts. She was beautiful, graceful, and she caused anxiety to stab my bowels. I was grateful when I followed Angel through the door to the dressing room. If I watched that dancer much longer, I would lose my nerve. I hoped the other girls weren't all like that one.

Embers, located about twenty miles from my home, was in a prime spot for out-of-town businessmen. Close to the airport and corresponding hotels and convention center, it wasn't any wonder that the club didn't have to try too hard to get customers. All the guys I saw so far, didn't fit the pervert in a trench coat picture I had in my head. As an added bonus, it was the only club in town.

The dressing room smelled much better than the rest of the club. In fact, it smelled like a Victoria Secret boutique. There was fresh lilac colored paint on the walls, and the beige carpet looked new. Make-up tables complete with lighted mirrors and plush velveteen upholstered stools lined the room. In the corner I saw what looked like a small bathroom complete with a shower. Three girls sat at different tables, and they turned toward Angel and me as we walked in. They all wore matching looks of clandestine distain, or possibly fear as their eyes landed on the salty door lady.

"This is Honey, Lexus, and Jasmine," Angel spit as she turned and walked out. The faces of the dancers brightened as they watched her leave.

Honey, a blonde with a generous figure and even more generous lips spoke first.

"Hi there. You're cute. Don't worry we got you. Angel can be a bit of a pill, but most of the other girls are really cool. Just don't get on her bad side and you'll be fine."

"Yeah, I got a weird vibe, for sure. I tipped her and even complimented her hair, but she looked like she wanted to eat me alive."

Jasmine, a dark-haired Asian lady drew in a sharp breath through clenched teeth but said nothing.

"Ooo...yeah. That's a wig, she's really touchy about that. But keep tipping and avoid her if you can. She's been here since the dawn of time and pretty much hates all of the dancers," Honey said. She was growing on me quickly. Colleen was standing behind her and nodding her approval too. Honey shivered. "It's really drafty in here tonight."

"Don't worry about it, let's get you set up. And then we'll show you around," said Lexus a squat little brunette who seemed to be the oldest of the group, maybe mid-thirties. Her heavy eye make-up and thick fake lashes made her eyes look tiny, especially in comparison to her boobs. Her giant breasts were a wonder of physics. She appeared to be leaning backward to keep from toppling forward.

The nerves that Angel had stepped on were finally starting to settle a little bit. These chicks seemed really cool. Colleen drifted behind me making my skin prickle. I could feel her excitement through the chill. She oozed out of the room and left me alone. Presumably to scope out the rest of the joint.

Honey showed me an empty spot at one of the make-up tables. I took out the gear I bought and started to dress. When I was ready, Lexus took me around the club floor, where I was a little dismayed to see that the patrons weren't looking at me. But Jasmine had taken to the stage and was drawing their attention, so I tried not to take it personally.

We walked back to the VIP room, where the private dances were held.

"Here is where your money comes from. We are a small club, but as the only act in town and so close to the hotels, you don't have to do much to make a lot. It's not like Vegas where the competition can get stiff," she giggled, "and you have to do a lot more. It can be a little daunting at first. I have a regular here that already made my night, I'll hook you up with him after your first stage and show you the basics."

"Thank you for being so cool," I said to her, and really meant it.

I still had no clue if I was going to be able to pull this off or not. And come to think of it, I still had no clue where Colleen had gone off to. But the night felt full of promise.

The last stop on our tour was the DJ booth. It was located on the side of the main room farthest from the stage. The middle-aged light-haired guy working the controls eyed me with obvious cynicism. I gave him a sheepish smile and prepared myself for an unpleasant encounter.

"First night?" he said but didn't give me a chance to answer. "You have two song sets, keep your top on for the first one, and take it off on the second. Don't leave the stage until you see the next girl coming. And don't linger if you see she is there. I'll give you a two-set warning before your turn. If you are in the VIP room, I will skip your turn. Tips are not technically mandatory, but you don't look dumb. You get how that works, I'm sure. Some DJs are real dicks if you don't tip whether you make money or not. I'm not one of those guys. Some nights will be great, others will suck. We take care of each other when we can in this shithole. I'm Lars, what kind of music do you like?"

Relieved that his cynicism was job and not people related I said, "Lars? Like the Metallica drummer?"

He rolled his eyes, "No Lars like my parents couldn't come up with anything better. You're a metal fan? Great."

"I am. I like the harder stuff. I don't know what to pick though."

"No worries, I got you. You got two sets, then you're up. What's your name?"

"Lilith," I said, feeling a little silly and wondering if I would remember my own fake name.

"Perfect. You'll do fine. These guys want boobs and someone to pay attention to them. Everything after that is pretty much unnecessary."

Honey gave him a head nod as we walked back into the dressing room. Once in there my anxiety came roaring back and I wondered where Colleen was. I needed her to get through this. And true to form, albeit not a solid one, she slithered through the door.

"You got this. It will be easy breezy beautiful…Covergirl… I promise," she said.

As much as I wanted to reply, I couldn't without looking like a total weirdo. I just looked at her with wide eyes, that I hoped showed how scared I was. She put a cold hand on my shoulder, and I felt just a little better. The song of the girl before me was ending, and I took one more look in the mirror before getting up to make my stripper debut.

"And now we welcome, for the first time ever, the enchanting Lilith!"

I stepped out onto the stage and into a cloud of fake smoke and colored lights. I wobbled on my heels and went straight to the pole to have something to hold on to. With the threat of falling mitigated, I felt better. I closed my eyes and started feeling myself and the music Lars had picked, a crunchy metal band I hadn't heard of with a female vocalist. When I opened them, I saw that my tip rail was full. Every guy in the place was staring and cheering and holding up money.

Colleen stood just beyond the stage grinning.

6

"Give it up for Lilith, a born natural. Can you believe that was her first time! Wow, I think we're going to keep her!" Lars belted.

Every guy sitting around the stage stood up and cheered. I looked at the aftermath of my first stage ever, and wondered how I would collect the bills that blanketed my stage. But I didn't have to wonder very long, as a very large, and very handsome dark-skinned bouncer appeared on stage with a broom. He nodded at me as he began to sweep up the money. I curtsied my audience, who reacted with more cheers, and made my exit.

Colleen greeted me backstage and threw her ghostly arms around me, making me shiver all the way around.

"You fucking killed it!"

"It was actually kind of fun."

It wasn't just kind of fun; it was damn near miraculous. The bouncer stepped off stage and handed me a plastic bucket filled with my spoils. I got a better look at him, and my knees almost buckled. He looked like a statue, a work of art in the flesh.

"Thank you," I said awkwardly. I felt a burst of cold behind me, Colleen had noticed him too.

"You really did great out there. Good job little lady, I'm Dominic, but you can call me Dom."

Oh, can I? I thought as another burst of cold came from behind me, blowing my hair forward.

"Sorry. I don't know what is up with this draft in here tonight."

"Uh, it's ok. I don't mind the cold. Thanks again."

Honey walked up as Lars started to introduce her, "You're going to do just fine, good job!" She said.

I smiled at her as she stepped out on her own stage and applause. None of this was what I had expected. I figured I would look like a goofball, and earn a few pity dollars, but this was nuts. Plus, all the girls were really nice so far. Angel of course being the exception. But I thought I could manage her. I was used to bullies. And this wasn't elementary school.

I barely finished that thought when Angel walked up holding some paperwork.

"New girls always do well at first. It doesn't last, but who knows, maybe you'll get lucky and find someone who really thinks you're pretty," she snarled through the approximation of a smile as she thrust the papers into my hands. "Fill these out and give them to Rick with your ID."

Colleen stuck her tongue out at her as she walked away. I was going to give her the finger, but Colleen stopped me.

"Nope, not the way to play that one. I poked around some, and up in the office her picture is all over. It appears that she is Queen Shit of this turd mountain. I certainly don't get her appeal, but it looks like she pretty much runs this place. The managers and owner seem to be wrapped around her finger."

"Maybe she's one of the alien lizard people?" I smirked.

"Or part of the ilumiTWATi." Colleen retorted, and we both broke into laughter.

We were still laughing when I carried my bucket of bills and paperwork into the dressing room. Jasmine was just leaving and looked at me a little weirdly as she walked out. I really need to remember not to laugh when no one else hears the joke. I looked at the paperwork Angel had handed me. It was a standard contract except for the parts where it forbade me to rub my bare genitals on the patrons. A condition I thought I could manage. I looked around for a pen, but Colleen was way ahead of me, and one rolled right under my hand. I signed it and fished my driver's license out of my bag.

I wasn't sure what to do with my bucket of money, leaving it in the dressing room didn't seem wise. Not even with my guardian spirit to stand guard, so I brought it with me. I found Rick back at the bar. Angel seemed to have gone back to her stool. I handed him the contract and my ID.

"Thanks, so we require at least three shifts a week, two of them need to be weeknights. I'm going to make a copy of your ID, then you can hit the floor." He walked away back behind the bar and into a room that I assumed was the office.

"Can I get you a water or something?" the pale and hopelessly freckled bartender asked. He was short and kind of pudgy but had kind eyes.

"I would love some. I'm Lace….. uh….Lilith."

He handed me a bottle of water and said, "Nice to meet you, I'm Pete."

An icepick jabbed me in the shoulder, and I turned to see Colleen nodding at my bucket of cash. I plucked out a few dollar bills and placed them on the bar. Pete smiled as he whisked them away.

"If you count out your tips into piles of twenties, I can exchange them for bigger bills if you would like. That makes them easier to carry. Some girls carry little purses or fold them into a band around their ankles. I wouldn't leave it in the dressing room. Our girls are really cool, but we get new people all the time and you never know."

I thanked him and began to count out my dollar bills. Rick came back out of the back room.

"Here's your license," he almost whispered.

I glanced at Colleen who was looking at him intensely. I wanted to ask her why but stayed quiet. I thanked him and he walked away. When I finished with my bills, I found that I had over $200 in one-dollar bills with about fifteen left over. Pete swept the piles up with a grin and replaced them as promised along with two rubber bands. I put one of them around my ankle, folded my money over it, and secured it with the other. Satisfied that it was safe, I smiled at Pete and walked back to the dressing room.

Honey was waiting for me, "Ok love, are you ready to learn to lap dance?"

I said yes, although I wasn't sure I was ready at all. She led me to her customer in the VIP room as promised. He was a middle-aged guy with thinning hair that wore a pot belly under an extra-large gray sweatshirt. He smelled like burning leaves and patchouli.

"This is Roger," Honey said.

Roger held his hand out and I shook it, "I'm Lilith."

"I'm going to do the first song, then you do the second," Honey said as she removed her blue sequined top. She sat in Roger's lap and moved her butt around some before turning around and smashing her boobs in his face. It looked easy enough.

When it was my turn, I copied her. I was caught off guard by Roger's erection but tried to hide my dismay.

"I think he likes you," Colleen said, and I rolled my eyes at her.

The song ended and Roger handed me my money which I tucked away with the rest. The rest of the night went really easy. A couple of customers came up to me and I did a few more lap dances and a few more stages. Dare I say, I enjoyed it. I know Colleen did. I had to ask her to stay back a little bit, because she kept making my legs prickly.

At the end of the night, I tipped out Lars, and made my way back to the dressing room. The girl who was on stage when I first came in was getting dressed too. She didn't say anything, so I didn't either. As I left, Dom picked up my stuff and I was grateful that he couldn't see Colleen mad dogging him as he walked me to my car. I thanked him and handed him a few bills. He smiled and I melted.

Colleen slid in next to me as I started the car. She was silent. Giving me the cold shoulder, it seemed. Literally and figuratively.

"Well, that was one of your better ideas," I said trying to break the chill. We both knew what or who the problem was. I love her, but her jealousy was hard to deal with sometimes.

"Dom was sure nice," she said looking like she just got a whiff of rotting fish.

"You got to let me like other people. Hey, it's not like he's a ghost. And besides, he knows I have to tip him. How will I ever really know if he even likes me," I was rambling.

"Whatever. Sure." Colleen was having none of it.

We drove home in the silence of our first spat. Richard was waiting as usual when we got back. He howled when I walked in the door, obviously near death from starvation. I filled his dish and tried to figure out how to make nice with my ghost.

I showered the stench of horny men off of me and got ready for bed. I was exhausted and thought I would drop off to sleep the second I closed my eyes. My whole body felt like it had been put through a woodchipper. My knees were raw from the stage, and I would see bruises the next day. Colleen was solid and already in bed when I got there. She had my computer open and was watching something. Her mood seemed to have improved.

"Did you know that the moon landing was a hoax?" She said. She was naked.

"Well, yes, of course," I replied. "Orchestrated by NASA to sell T-shirts. Duh,"

I slid into bed, and she closed the laptop and set it on the nightstand. I leaned in and kissed her. She hesitated and kissed me back. I found I could stay awake just a little longer.

7

Colleen

So… I get a little jealous…I'm a demon not a saint. And he is a spectacular hunk of man meat, so I guess it is a little hard to blame her. But still. Lacey is mine. I don't want to share. Jealous and selfish, but again. Demon. A helpful demon, but still a demon. And there's another thing I haven't really wanted to tell Lacey. As a succubus, I need semen to survive. So not quite a ghost, not quite a liar, but most likely a cum demon. Fun right?

Except that when I engage humans in sex acts to obtain said cum, sometimes they die. Well usually they die. Hence Mary. Which I swear was an accident. In my defense, I didn't think I could kill a woman that way. I figured it was just guys. When I can, I go out looking on my own when she's sleeping. I try to make it quick and easy. And not too often. But you know, a girl's got to eat. I'm not sure that all of my lovers or ours if I'm involved, will survive the encounter, so the last thing I need is Lacey catching feelings.

And ultimately, I have a bigger concern. Angel. That's not her real name as far as I can tell. Unless her parents named her that to be funny because she was born with horns and a tail. There is nothing funny at all about her. There is something profoundly wrong with her. I haven't figured it out, but I will. I wasn't lying about her being the lynchpin of that club. When I snooped around the office, I found some stuff. Angel was one of the first dancers to work there. She doesn't seem to be married to the owner or manager, but they seem to almost worship her. Or are afraid of her. An advantage to being immaterial is that I can look through closed doors. But what I found in one of the cabinets was disturbing, even to me.

I told Lacey that I had seen Angel's picture, which is true, but what I saw was more of an altar. A sort of shrine to that awful lady. Half burned candles and incense surrounding what must be a really outdated picture of her. The bones of what I think may have been a hamster lay in a smattering of ashes. As if it were an offered sacrifice. Now I think I would know if Angel were a supernatural being of some sort. While I've yet to meet another demon on earth, I think I would recognize my own kind.

I do love a good conspiracy, and I am frankly fascinated by what humans make up for attention online, and some of it is very convincing. Plausible. I'm sure some of it is true even and I love following the clues. But mostly what I do when I'm looking at Lacey's computer is trying to learn about myself and what the hell I am. That's how I came to see myself as a succubus, or sex demon. Although all of the information I have found is buried in contradictory myths and folklore. Much of it is from ancient texts from many different cultures and religion. And a whole lot from books and movies. Honestly, I'm not convinced that any of them are accurate at all. Maybe just bits and pieces of truth muddled with made up stuff. But I'm pretty good at picking out good information. One thing I learned is that when a succubus is in love, their partner won't die. So, there's that at least. I'm becoming a very good researcher and parsing the truth from fiction.

As a succubus, I have certain powers of persuasion. And horny men are kind of my jam, a necessity actually. Which is a big reason why I suggested this particular line of work for my love. Not that she wouldn't have done alright without me, but a little grease in the wheels never hurts. I can't completely manipulate men or sometimes women, I can just influence them in the general direction I want them to move in. There's the whole dream sex cum death thing.

I can't read thoughts, but I can get a general sense of what someone is thinking. It's how I come to *know* things. Being able to sneak around unseen helps a lot too. Like that Dom really does like Lacey. But as much as I would like him to be a bad guy, as far as I can tell he isn't. The bastard. Rick was easy to read at first, but something got in the way when Lacey gave him her paperwork. In that moment, I couldn't nudge him either. And part of me, well, all of me really suspects it has something to do with that door girl.

There's a lot I don't know about myself and my existence. I don't know if I can't remember or if maybe I didn't exist until I showed up and attached to Lacey. I was telling the truth when I told Lacey that I felt a pulling or sucking feeling and then just showed up. Was I being born? Or simply pulled from my own realm? And I really have no idea how to get back or if I really even want to. Hell, I can't be certain there is a place to go back to. I like it here. I love Lacey, and there is so much to learn and discover. And besides I don't seem to have much of a choice anyway. Might as well enjoy it.

8

I woke up sweating. Richard was snuggled up next to me where Colleen should be. I threw the blankets off without disturbing the cat. He lay there as if nothing had happened, snoring slightly. I rubbed his head, and he kept snoring. I don't like waking up without her. Partly because all of my blankets are just too much without her coolness to mitigate the heat. But mostly I don't like waking up without her because I am afraid that she will disappear as suddenly as she appeared. At least it isn't all that often. Maybe once or twice a month. And I always find her poking around on the computer when she's not in bed. Richard didn't mind her being gone of course. As far as I know he is the only one that can see her. And Richard is not a fan.

I sat up and swung my legs off the side of the bed, but when I tried to stand, I almost fell over. The pain in my muscles was intense. I looked down at my knees. The dark purple that had appeared overnight would have been pretty if it weren't so painfully ugly. As I sat back down, Colleen entered the bedroom with a swoosh holding two steaming mugs of coffee, which she almost dropped when she saw my knees.

"Oh no! That looks like it hurts. It also looks kind of cool," she handed me my coffee which she had put in my favorite mug which had pink and purple flowers surrounding the words 'Fuck off' on it. She set her own mug down on the nightstand and kneeled before me, placing her hands on my knees. Her cold hands soothed my skin.

"Dude, that feels so good."

"It's a good thing you don't have to go back in tonight. Let's spend the day in bed," she wore a mischievous smile and nothing else. Spending the day in bed is Colleen's panacea. And I have to admit it's not a bad one, not sure if it actually cures anything, but I'm also not sure that really matters.

"Have you been up for a while?"

"Not too long. Just doing some googling," she said. But something about the way she said it made me curious. Usually, she can't wait to tell me what profound discovery she had made in the dark depths of the internet. In fact, I can't remember if I have ever had to ask at all.

"Anything interesting?"

"You know the usual. Ooooh....I did see that the global elites are going to put out a signal from the 5G cell towers. It will activate the microchips that they have been putting into vaccines. It will make everyone slaves. Mind control. I'm not all that worried."

"My parents took me to get them when I was a kid."

"No worries, I'm pretty sure I can protect you. I think. It won't be until JFK Jr comes back so we might have a while."

"I mean he's pretty dead, so I think we're good."

Colleen looked away and I couldn't shake the sense that there was something she wasn't telling me. I've gotten used to a certain amount of not-knowing with my ghost companion. I know she doesn't tell me everything, and for the most part I'm cool with that. But there is a part of me that wonders if she isn't who she says she is. I've always thought that she is either protecting me or herself. Obviously, there is something in her past she doesn't want to tell me, or maybe I'm just being paranoid. This is definitely not how I imagined my life going, this strange relationship with a ghost. Not to mention the whole stripper thing. How the hell did I let her talk me into that anyway? She seems to have certain powers of persuasion over people. I like to think that I am immune to them, but she's really convincing sometimes. Well, all the time.

I heard the whoosh of air brakes outside and stepped to the bedroom window and spread the curtains. Across the street, a large truck was parked in front of the black carcass of Mary's house. The truck produced a loud beeping noise as the flat bed tilted up to unload a huge dumpster. Yellow caution tape crisscrossed the front door, which to me looked more like a formality than anything else. Not even the most determined hoodlum would dare to enter what was left of the structure. From the street it was obvious that there wasn't anything of value left in it.

"Looks like they're getting ready to tear down Mary's house," I said.

Colleen let out a distracted grunt, and when I turned around to climb back into bed, she was frowning at the computer screen.

"Ok, I'm done wondering. What is up?"

"Not anything major, I'm sure," she said, and I didn't believe her. "I was just looking to see if I could find anything out about our new friend Angel."

"That chick sucks for sure. She is sweet as pie to the guys, but a total cunt to everyone else. She's probably just jealous of the dancers."

"She's a regular Dr. Jekyll and Mrs. Cuntface," she said her frown disappearing as she closed her laptop and looked up at me. Coffee shot out of my nose and we both began to laugh.

My laugh turned into giggles before fading, "Well now I got to wash the sheets again."

"Since they're dirty anyway," Colleen said looking at me under her eyelashes. I swear I have no willpower with her. Richard, who had relocated to the foot of the bed, snarled at Colleen before hopping down before he could be annoyed any further.

"See ya later Dick!" Colleen said before turning her attentions towards me. I let her have her way, as always. Although, I can't say I've ever put up much of a fight.

Colleen had a way of making me forget, well just about everything. When our fun was over our coffee had long gone cold. I had almost fallen back asleep, I drifted in a wave of afterglow and on the edge of dreams. A loud knock at the door brought me back and sent my heart racing. I was exhausted from the night before, not to mention our recent activities. So once the initial shock of the noise wore off, I started to drift again. It had to be some salesperson or something, and I was happy right where I was.

But then it came again, louder. And this time it scared me. Whoever was at my door was pounding on it like they weren't going to go away. Now I was annoyed. And alarmed. I got up and threw on a long T-shirt and nothing else. I caught a glance at my appearance in my bedroom mirror as I half limped to the front door. My knees were a sight to behold, blue and purple bruises covered both of them. I looked like a little kid who had fallen off her bike a dozen times. Although, when you combined it with my wild bedhead and the stubborn remnants of the eyeliner that hadn't washed off in the shower, I looked more like a lady who had spent the night earning her rent money in an alley behind a dumpster. I hoped I would scare whoever was trying to beat my door in.

I was still a few steps away from the door, when the pounding came for a third time, and I saw the silhouette of a person trying to peer into the window through the closed blinds. Now I was pissed. If this guy was trying to sell me a vacuum, I was going to lose it. I opened the door with a flourish and was about to yell at the offending door knocker, but then I saw the badge, and instantly deflated.

"Uh….Hello, can I help you?" I said lamely. He was dressed in a dark blue, or maybe dark gray suit and I was looking at my wild reflection in his aviator sunglasses. He might have been handsome, but my crotch had crawled up into my lungs and snuggled up against my hammering heart, so I couldn't be sure. I reminded myself that I had no real reason to freak out, and that helped a little. Not that much though, because he was holding his badge up in front of my face and I saw that he wasn't a regular cop. He was a homicide cop. The cold draft that was my lover drifted in behind me, but Colleen said nothing. I offered a lame smile.

"Sorry to bother you Miss." I got the distinct impression that he wasn't sorry at all, "My name is Detective Shelton, and I have a few questions about your late neighbor Mary. May I come in?" He smiled.

9

I wished that the thin T-shirt I had thrown on covered more of my legs. Especially because Colleen was so close to me. I was shivering. Shaking in front of a cop who wants to ask questions about a dead old lady and possible arson couldn't be a good look. I also wished in that moment that my shirt didn't read "I'm not a gynecologist, but I'll take a look" a souvenir from a Mr. Right Now, I had found at the bar. I should have returned it to him and *really* should have looked at what I was throwing on to answer the door. Not that I was embarrassed, but I was really fucking up this whole first impression thing.

"Um, my house is a real mess right now. Can you let me put on some pants and we can talk outside?" I said, glancing toward the bong and huge bag of weed sitting on my coffee table. It's not illegal, but still.

"No!" Colleen yelled in my ear, and my whole body broke out in gooseflesh. "Invite him in. People that smoke weed have terrible memories. And a terrible memory could come in handy." She had a point.

"This could take a little while, and it would be better to sit down," he said, ignoring the two chairs sitting on my porch, but obviously noticing my shirt. I hoped he was just trying to check out my boobs, but somehow, I doubted that.

"Ok, give me a few minutes to tidy up and get dressed," I smiled as I shut the door in his face.

I looked at Colleen, who wore a blank expression. She went solid and started to pick up some stuff in the living room. Sweeping the pot crumbs off the coffee table and moving the drug paraphernalia to a spot in the corner where it could be observed but wasn't on display. She is so smart. Meanwhile I ran into my room and threw on some sweatpants. My hair screamed the fact that I had just gotten laid, and I tried to quiet it with a scrunchie. But that only had the effect of making it look like I had just gotten laid and then put my hair in a ponytail. I didn't bother changing my shirt. That ship had sailed.

I looked at my ghost partner and asked quietly, "Should we make some coffee or something? Offer him something to drink?"

She shook her head no, and faded until I could see the front door through her. She nodded her head for me to open the door and gave me a look that said she would be right there with me. Seriously, I wonder sometimes how I ended up so lucky to have wound up with her. I opened the door just as Detective Shelton drew back from trying to peer into the front window again. He looked slightly embarrassed, and I smiled at him. Grateful for the brief feeling of having the upper hand in this situation. I had a moment to wonder if maybe I was overreacting to his sudden inquiry. I mean, the house had burned down with a person in it. It made total and complete sense that someone would be asking some questions.

"Please come in," I said and opened the door to let him in. I swept my arm toward the sofa my mother had purchased shortly before she passed. He glanced at Richard who was perched on one arm of it, eyeing the detective suspiciously. Judging by how much he hates Colleen, I'm not sure how much I trust his judgement. But it was nice to feel like he had my back in this situation.

"Thank you," Detective Shelton said as he took a seat. I saw his gaze land on the bong in the corner and Colleen gave me an enthusiastic thumbs up from the corner of the room.

"Would you like something to drink? I think I have some lemonade, or I can make some coffee if you would like?" I said, totally forgetting that I wasn't supposed to do that. At least the pot making for a bad memory wasn't a lie.

Colleen shook her head violently and said, "No we don't want him to hang out too long!"

"No thank you," he said, and I let out my breath. Fuck I was really bad at this. "Ok, so you've lived here for some time. How long did you know the deceased?" He removed a notepad and pen from the inside pocket of his suit jacket.

"Well, my mom knew her better than I did. But we were friendly. She seemed like a nice lady. She went to bible study almost every week. And gave us Christmas cookies every year."

"Mmm….bible study?" he said as scribbled something down. "Her family said she wasn't all that religious. Are you sure that was where she went every week?"

"Well, I guess not. Now that I think of it. I just assumed that's where she went. Maybe a book club or something?"

"Something like that," he said, and his tone stabbed me in the stomach. Colleen put her hand straight in the air like a Nazi salute. She drifted up behind him to peer over his shoulder at his notebook and her eyebrows raised and she gave me a sheepish smile.

"Do you remember the last time you spoke with her?"

I looked up to the ceiling, honestly trying to remember and failing, "I really don't remember. She was kind of just in the neighborhood and we didn't talk all that often. No real reason to." I shifted my eyes to the weed to bolster the credibility of my bad memory. Despite the fact that I was telling the truth.

Detective Shelton scribbled again on his pad and shivered as Colleen bent closer to read his writing. He looked around as if trying to find a draft. "Do you know of anyone who might have been angry with her?"

"Not at all. She was just a nice old lady." I didn't want to mention the Nazi stuff, even though I suppose that could make someone angry with her. And how would I know about the Nazi stuff unless I had been digging around in her closets? Ok, maybe I was getting better at this.

"Ok. So, you weren't all that close with her. Would you say maybe you only saw her once or twice a week?"

"Yes, about that. Mostly we just waved from across the street. I pretty much keep to myself anyway."

"But you do like to go out? A young lady like yourself?"

"Well, yes, I go out sometimes," this was taking a weird turn. Colleen was staring at me from across the room.

"But no boyfriend? That's an interesting shirt you have there. Do you remember where you got it?" Was he hitting on me?

"Um….I got it from a friend."

"I see. Well…I think that's about all I have for now. We really just have a few loose ends to tie up before they start the demolition. Are you planning on going out of town anytime soon? I may have another question or two." He closed up his notebook and stowed it back into his suit pocket along with the pen.

"No, I'm not planning on going anywhere. I just started a new job," I said and immediately regretted it, but felt better about it when he didn't ask me to elaborate. I can't imagine that strippers had a lot of credibility in the eyes of law enforcement. Just a hunch.

Detective Shelton stood up and reached into his pocket and pulled out a business card. He handed it to me as he turned to the front door. I walked him out and said goodbye. As I shut the door behind him, I turned to Colleen who was solid again.

"I think that went ok. What was he writing?"

"It went great. Just some notes, nothing serious," she said, but I wasn't sure I believed her all the way.

"Kind of weird he asked about my shirt though." I said.

Colleen just nodded, kissed me, and said, "Let's go forget about it."

She led me to our bedroom, and I did.

10

Colleen

I don't know how serious it was, maybe just a little. According to that cop's notes, it would appear that Mary wasn't a Nazi after all. But a collector and World War II buff. My bad. It wasn't bible study she had been going to, but a history club. I stand by my statement though. She was old and I'm sure she's better off now. Well pretty sure anyway.

But that's not what's freaking me out. It's the shirt. He hadn't been making any notes about Mary, although he is investigating that too, he had the name of the bar that we had gone to where we met the owner of that ridiculous shirt. How he made the connection I'm not sure. I will need to find out, but telling Lacey any of that right now won't help anything. Plus, I have this all under control. Mostly anyway.

A few months back, Lacey and I had gotten bored. I might have been just a little hungry also, so we decided to go out to the local bar here in town. In hindsight, I should have suggested one a little farther away. Lacey doesn't drink, she was looking for some male companionship. If only briefly. I played invisible wing man and helped her pick out a guy that would do the trick. So, to speak.

Anyway, like I said, Lacey doesn't drink so she just ordered a soda with a twist. That way it looked like she was drinking. For some reason guys at the bar tend to be a little suspicious of ladies that aren't drinking. Lacey had eaten a weed edible earlier, so she was feeling good.

This guy named Scott, came up and started talking. He had short blond hair and just a hint of a beard. Dressed in a T-shirt and cargo shorts, he might have been just a tad douchey, but we weren't looking for marriage material anyway. Which he definitely wasn't. In fact, I could see or sense maybe that he wasn't a great guy. I think he sold mortgages or something or something shady. And well… Lacey, ended up back at his place.

I held back and waited, and yeah, I watched. Just to make sure everything was cool. And I needed to collect my semen too. You know so I don't die. But just as it was about to happen, Lacey had him in her mouth and well she ended up collecting it. Not an ideal situation. She had gotten hers first and so she was really just being nice. One of the reasons I love her. But it meant that I was left without my life-giving substance. So later, after she was home and in bed, I went back to pay Scott another visit.

He was sleeping and I really intended just to get him to….well you know…get what I needed and move on. I really didn't want to hurt the guy. Not at all. I just wanted to not die myself. I mean…without me, what would happen to Lacey? I really didn't have a choice. I was hoping if I was really gentle, he would be okay.

I got into his dreams, which were super weird. Something about a hamster and a bucket of oil, no matter what it wasn't cool. I turned his dream in a different direction, and he became aroused. I got a little carried away, and I got what I wanted. Needed. When I was finished, I looked over at him and he was just staring at the ceiling. I figured he was fine. His eyes were totally open. Although so was his mouth. It was open in what looked like a scream of ecstasy. A terrified, horrible scream of orgasm. But then I noticed that he wasn't breathing anymore. Totally not my fault. At least I don't think. But like I said I think he was kind of a douche anyway. He had some kind of pills in his pocket. What if they were roofies or something? I bet they were. Roofies. He was a bad guy. Probably.

I left and went back. It's not like I didn't feel bad. In fact, instead of getting back in bed with Lacey, I opened her computer to do some more research. I wanted to see if I could find any more information about Succubae. Maybe find a way to not kill but still collect the semen. That was when I learned that love stops the death thing. So, I just need to love more. I may be a demon, but that doesn't mean I can't work on myself. Lucky for me, there's a ton of stuff out there on how to work on relationships.

Back to Detective Shelton, I read his notes, and he seems to think there could be a connection between Mary and Scott's death. Totally ridiculous I know. Just because Lacey happened to know both of those people and they happen to be dead now. It's obviously just a coincidence.

11

I woke up alone. Again. And sweating. Richard was on top of me. He protested when I made him move, but I was about to boil to death in my own juices if I let him stay. I tossed the covers off me and reveled in the cool air of the room. I had been dreaming of some sort of reptile house, hundreds of snakes slithered around a sweltering and moist enclosure. Although, someone was there that I think was about to rescue me. I had started to panic, right before I woke up. I am not a fan of snakes. Stupid angry legless oversized worms. You would think with my love of horror and heavy metal that I would be into reptiles, but nope. I hate them.

I heard Colleen tapping away at the computer in the living room. It made me feel better to know that she wasn't far away. I laid there for a moment as my dream evaporated and my body cooled. The events from yesterday spooked me, but Colleen assured me that everything would be fine. I wanted to believe her, but there was something that didn't quite let me. It was his fixation on my shirt and asking about going out to the bar. I couldn't understand how that had anything to do with Mary or her death. I figured though

I was just being paranoid. It was a funny shirt, that was probably it.

I got out of bed all the way, I put on the flimsy blue robe that was hanging on the chair. Richard, assuming correctly, that I was headed to the kitchen where his dish was located, hopped off the bed to follow me. He darted out in front of me and straight to his bowl which was empty. Empty except for the half a cup of kibble that lined the bottom. He looked at me and meowed sweetly. Hoping to get me to fill his dish before making coffee. I complied. Ghosts and cats have a way of making me do that.

I yawned as I filled the carafe, put in a filter and filled it with way too much ground coffee. I like it thick, so I can dilute it with cream and sugar. Colleen blew in just as I pressed the start button.

"Oh hey, sorry. I was going to do that. I got kind of carried away. Did you know about the global cabal of celebrities that kidnap children and drain them of their adrenochrome?"

"You know, I didn't. Is it the scientologists? That would totally explain Tom Cruise."

"No silly. Scientology is totally made up, like all the religions," Colleen rolled her eyes. "Celebrities use adrenochrome to get high and stay famous."

"Good thing I don't want to be famous, I don't think harvesting children's adreno-whatever is my jam. I go back to work tonight."

The coffee pot started to gurgle and spit the last of its black nectar into the pot. I plucked our mugs out of the dishwasher and filled them up, diluting mine with sweetness.

"Are you nervous?"

"You know I thought I would be, but I'm not. My knees look pretty bad. Maybe we should go out and get some stockings or something to cover them up."

"Probably not a bad idea," she looked down where my robe left my legs exposed and cringed.

I jumped in the shower and got dressed. We had only a few hours before I was due for my shift. Despite my nightmare, I slept much later than I had thought I would. On the way out the door, I saw that the construction, or demolition crew had started to dismantle Mary's house. That eased my mind a little. More than a little really. I didn't think that the police would let them tear it down if they were still investigating.

Colleen was already in the front seat by the time I opened the door and started the car. Most of the time it was easy to forget that she was a ghost and not a real person. Except when she did stuff like that. Leaking through doors and windows and stuff. I'm not sure I'll ever get used to that.

We stopped at the same store where I bought my bikini. I found some thick thigh high stockings that would hide my wounded knees and hopefully provide some protection from the rough stage, so they didn't get worse. Colleen was once again mesmerized by the dildos. It was hard to blame her. The extra-large ones were a sight to behold. Although the jumbo butt plugs gave them a run for their money.

"Pretty pretty please can we take him home?" She said, although she was hard to understand with the end of an enormous dark blue rubber two headed dick with flecks of glitter embedded in it in her mouth. But I got the gist. I looked around to see if anyone had noticed. If they had, they would see a dildo floating in mid-air. It wasn't as big as the purple one she had found the first time we were here. And it was kind of pretty.

"Well ok. But only if you promise to feed and clean up after him."

The dildo popped out of her mouth, and she said with a huge grin, "I promise!"

We stopped at a diner so I could get some food before work. I ordered two cheeseburgers to go, and we ate them in the car. I'm not sure if Colleen even needs to eat, but she enjoys it. As I drove toward the club, I did start to get a little nervous. But then I remembered Colleen's powers of persuasion and felt better. I guess it is kind of like cheating.

We pulled up to the club and the parking lot where around a dozen other cars were parked. I suspected it would be a little busier than Tuesday night had been. Angel was sitting at the entrance as expected. And as expected, she was settling in for a night of making people uncomfortable.

"Hi, how are you tonight?" I said and immediately regretted it. Angel smiled a smile full of capped teeth and I recoiled.

"Just peachy," she replied through her smile, but her eyes gave me the impression she was smiling at the thought of my corpse. She was looking past me, and toward Colleen. My stomach dropped to my feet as the notion that she could see my companion hit me. My hand shook as I dropped a ten-dollar bill into her tip jar and walked into the bowels of the club. Colleen caught my vibe and said, "I know what that looked like, but I don't think she can see me." I shrugged indicating that I wasn't sure, not wanting to reply out loud.

With Colleen in tow, I passed Rick the manager who just nodded as I walked toward the dressing room. Lars was on his perch in the DJ booth, and he nodded at me too. I'm starting to think that is preferred greeting. I nodded back, feeling like part of the tribe. Just a quick head nod, no water cooler talk. I could dig it.

I pushed open the door to the dressing room and was immediately engulfed in a thick fragrant cloud of smoke. Not the fake kind that spews from the machine above the stage, but smoke from what seemed like a hundred burning sticks of incense. I aimed in the general direction of a stool at one of the make-up counters and hoped for the best, waving my hand to clear the air as I walked. A tickle appeared in my nose, and I tried to suppress a sneeze, but failed epically. The three other girls in the dressing, whom I couldn't identify due to the cloud said in unison, "Sorry".

"It's ok," I sniffled. "You find a dead rat in here or something?"

Someone turned on a fan, the smoke started to clear, and I saw that Jasmine, Honey and a lady I didn't recognize occupied the space.

"It's a sage smudging to get rid of the bad JuJu," Honey said.

The slender dark brunette who I didn't know yet looked like she had been crying. Then she sniffed and I knew that she had been crying. Her sniffing and red tipped nose really gave it away. I got up and extended my hand to her, which she took softly.

"I'm Lacey. Well. Lilith, I guess."

"I'm Taylor," she replied with her eyes down. She still held my hand, and it was getting awkward. I gently pulled my hand away and she sniffed again.

"You okay?"

Taylor sniffed again and Honey answered for her, "Just a little club drama, she'll be all right. We got her. You ready for another night? You really killed it last time."

Taylor didn't look all that all right to me, but I was starting to think it was a bunch of none of my business. I wondered what Colleen thought about it, she was the ghost in the room. Sometimes the hardest thing about having her around was not being able to talk to her in the moment.

I got ready and went about my night. My stages were great again, consistently. It was like card counting at a casino, I couldn't lose. I'm not a dummy though, I know that Colleen was influencing at least some of the patrons. I was so busy, that I was turning down lap dances. The other girls and staff had definitely noticed. More than one person let me know that it was new girl luck. Not in a mean way but inferring that it wouldn't last. And given my distinct lack of dancing skills, I thought it might not be a bad idea to tell Colleen to lay off lest it start to cause problems. I wanted attention from the customers, not the staff.

By the time Dom helped me to my car, my favorite part of the night, I felt like a sweaty gym towel. I tipped him, and he smiled at me sending shivers straight to my crotch. Almost like Colleen does, but warmer. As she drifted into the passenger seat, I could see she was dying to say something important. She had been eerily quiet the whole night, but I had figured that she had been busy helping me. Now she looked like she was going to burst.

As soon as Dom walked away Colleen blurted, "I know what's up with Angel…she's the leader of a death cult."

"What?" I said, as I started the car and started to pull away. "It might be time you lay off the YouTube videos."

"No really. The first time we were there I found this weird altar with her picture and stuff. A picture from when she was younger. She was one of the first dancers."

"We already knew all that though. I'm sure the older staff is just really attached to her. Or she's fucking the owner or manager or something. It's not all that surprising that an OG like her would have some pull at a little club like that."

"It's way more than that. You know that girl Taylor that was all upset tonight?" I nodded that I did, keeping my eyes on the road. "Well, I heard Rick and the bartender talking about Angel and they said that Taylor had refused to tip and that she might have to be taken out. They were talking about having to keep Angel happy or *things would get bad*."

"*Taken out?* Is she a cult leader or a mob boss? For real, she's a bitter bitch, but no one is killing anyone."

"The girls lit all that incense to purify her energy so she wouldn't be sacrificed," Colleen was close to sounding like the tomato face guy talking about lizard people. As much as I wanted to get off the subject and talk about something else, I had to know if Colleen thought that Angel could see her. That really would be a problem.

"People use sage all the time to clear out bad smells and stuff," the sacrifice thing was nuts. "Someone probably just had some bad fish or something. It did look like Angel might have been looking at you. Do you think she can see you like I can?"

Colleen paused. "I'm not sure. I don't think so. I don't think she has supernatural powers or anything. I really think I would know if she did. But the cult leaders don't need actual powers to manipulate their followers."

That was true. The internet is full of goofy people saying goofy things to people who want to believe them.

"Well, I just got this job, and I kind of like it. I don't even know how far away the next club is. What would we do if that were true anyway?"

"I guess I don't know. But we should be careful anyway." She was sulking now. As much as I trust her, I have to remind myself that she is…was…human and capable of being wrong and mislead. But a ton of smart people have gone down rabbit holes of bullshit. One second, you're watching silly cat videos and the next you're wearing tin foil panties to keep the pussy gnomes away.

"We will, I promise." It was weird to see her so worked up, but until someone actually dies, I can't say I was all that worried.

And then, someone did.

12

Colleen

I know she thinks I'm nuts. Maybe I am. But then again maybe not. I have taught myself how to research on the internet. There is a vast amount of information if you know where to look. And I don't need a degree. I'm a supernatural creature for fuck's sake. I'm sure I'm better equipped to navigate all the bullshit than any human.

Although, it does seem to be draining my energy. I'll need to feed again soon. Getting Lacey a job at the strip club has got to be one of my very best ideas. Not only can I pretty much guarantee that she makes a ton of money, negating the need to break into and burn down the houses of not-so-nazi old ladies, but I think I will have access to an ungodly amount of semen. My strip club research does show that strip club customers aren't really supposed to get off, but who the fuck are they fooling? That must happen. And my hope is that if I catch it while they are awake, I won't kill them in the process. Seriously, I impress myself sometimes.

I got off track thinking about cum, my bad. Angel is the real problem here. She is a death cult leader. Her followers believe that the end of the world is coming and that she is going to be the one to save them. Now that part is obviously bullshit, but it only really matters what they do with that information. I think she is getting people to kill people they think are impeding that goal. Which in Angel's case, are people she has decided are evil. My guess is that it's just people that piss her off. Like Taylor. I'll bet that she won't be there the next time Lacey goes to work.

How can I be so sure? Well, I found the podcast she uses to seduce people with conspiracy theories. Back in the day she may have used video, but these days, the camera is not her friend. Honestly, I think that is at the heart of all this. Her deep-seated insecurities and jealousy. Pride and envy of biblical proportions or maybe she's just psychotic. Whatever, she is a bad mama. Obviously, she has the club staff and owners wrapped around her fingers and so far, I think it is really just the male staff. The girls are afraid of her. I'm almost positive that she is just a human who is particularly good at manipulation. A con artist.

I also found out that she isn't just one of the first dancers turned deified door girl, but she is also the bookkeeper. There could be a financial incentive to keeping the staff in line. Oh yeah, she's a bad person. I think that Lacey is safe for now, but I can't imagine she will be for long. Especially if she keeps cleaning up like she does. Angel will notice if she hasn't already and turn her attention to Lacey before long, I'm sure of it. And I will be here to protect her.

I know she doesn't believe just yet, but Lacey will come around.

13

We drove the rest of the way home in silence. Again. Colleen didn't seem to be stewing so much as thinking. Since she came into my life, we have spent most of our time laughing and goofing off. Getting into and out of trouble together. I wasn't used to this kind of stuff with her. If it were a real relationship, I might consider couple's therapy. But that doesn't seem like a viable option given the whole ghost thing.

When I opened the door, Richard was waiting just inside. It was something like three in the morning, so I guess he was extra salty. He meowed at me in greeting, but it morphed into a spastic hiss when he saw Colleen. He ran out of the room and into the kitchen.

"Well fuck you very much, Dick," Colleen said, but the fun was gone from her voice. I knew I needed to do something to lighten the mood a little. I thought I would try one of her tricks.

"Hey, what do you say after I rinse off, we try out your new buddy we got at the dirty store. You know blue *is* my favorite color," I smiled as I finished the sentence.

"I need to show you something first," she said, her tone was still unsettling. I relented.

"Ok."

She opened the laptop and clicked immediately on a tab she had bookmarked. Up popped a podcast called Dark Angel. It wasn't hard to see where this was going. But I humored her in the hopes that I might be able to lead her out of her conspiratorial thinking. She clicked play on the last episode. A gravelly voice began to speak. It might have been a female voice, but they were using some sort of device to make it unidentifiable. Like murder documentaries do when they are hiding a witness's identity.

As I listened, I began to see what Colleen was talking about. The voice, whoever they were, was talking about the end of the world. They were talking about the need to sacrifice those who have spoken against them. Supposedly these people were part of a global cabal plotting to take over the world in the name of Satan and prevent the second coming. And that if those people weren't *taken out* before the end came, their people would be among the damned. And the voice was also selling magic amulets of protection. Apparently facilitating the end of the world and the second coming of Christ was dangerous and expensive. In fact, they had certificates of salvation for sale also, just to make sure that their precious followers would be double saved. It was quite the racket.

The voice started to talk about the evils of sexual desire and how evil women exploit men to ensure they end up in hell. Ok, so now I was starting to get it. The more I listened, the more I came to understand what had Colleen's panties in knot. Just kidding, Colleen doesn't wear panties. Or a bra for that matter. She was staring at me as I listened, her cold stare unnerving. It actually made me just a little afraid of her. And that had never happened before.

"Do you see now? I don't think she's supernatural, I just think she's found a lucrative way to manipulate people. She is feeding her ego and lining her pockets at the same time," Colleen looked at me hopefully. Which was way better than how she had been looking at me.

"Yeah, I see. I guess I'm not totally convinced this is the same Angel. But it is compelling. What would we be able to do about it anyway? We don't know that she is really doing anything bad, other than running a bit of a scam that plays on the people's fear and gullibility."

She looked at me and conceded, "I guess nothing," she said sounding just a little defeated. I think she was more concerned that I believed her than what Angel might be up to. That was encouraging, because I figured it was the validation of her own conclusion she was looking for. I hoped that this would be the end of the weirdness between us. And then she gave me that look from under eyelashes, that confirmed what I was thinking. "So, we haven't given him a name yet." Her mischievous smile was back, and it hit me below the belly button.

"Why don't you think about it, while I get cleaned up?"

Ready to move on from this whole Satanic Cabal bullshit, I rinsed off quickly. Colleen was waiting on the bed when I got out of the shower.

"Bert! Let's call him Bert," she said wiggling the gelatinous glittery dildo. "It's got two heads though."

"How about one head we call Burt and the other Ernie?"

"Clever." She said as she slipped the towel off me. She took my left nipple into her cool mouth, and I moaned.

"I think I like Bert. He can stay," I breathed when we were done.

"I'm a fan of Ernie too," Colleen smiled and kissed me again.

"I think I'm going to need another shower though," I kissed her back and slipped out of my cool bed and into a warm shower.

To my utter dismay, Colleen was back on the laptop while I smeared make-up on in preparation for my third night as a stripper. It was a Friday and my first weekend night. I had been so busy already on the slow nights, and my nerves were working themselves into a frenzy. People in large numbers were not my thing. Neither were people in small numbers. So maybe it was just people that weren't my thing. Dom strode into my thoughts like a dark cowboy into an old saloon, and my nerves electrified. I had a vague sense that he had been in my dreams. Dreams I couldn't remember. I made a mental note to make sure I got to talk to him again.

We pulled into the parking lot of the illustrious Embers Gentleman's Club around eight. The cars were sparse, giving me hope that it wouldn't be too crowded after all. Angel growled a greeting at the door, although she looked slightly brighter than she had. I wondered if she had gotten laid. I almost asked then thought better of it. I had learned back in middle school that bullies had a habit of simply disappearing if you didn't give them any fuel. At least the worst of my bullies did. Vivian was pure malice in the flesh, and one day she just wasn't there.

Angel was still here though, and that sucked. I gave her a sticky sweet smile and dropped a ten in her jar. Colleen flipped her off for me. The gesture had two meanings. First a real fuck you to the super cunt, and second to see if she would react to the obvious afront. Unless she was really good at hiding her anger, Angel gave no indication that she saw it. Looking at her, it wasn't hard to see her as a manipulative cult leader. As she spoke, I heard a vague resemblance to the voice on the podcast. I still had a kernel of doubt, but it was shrinking as we completed our brief interaction.

The customer count on the main floor reflected the cars in the parking lot. The dressing room was a different story though. It was packed with naked bodies. A few I recognized and many more that I didn't. I looked around for Taylor and didn't see her. Colleen noticed her absence too and elbowed me and made me shiver.

"See, I bet she's dead," she whispered in my ear. I gave her a look that I hoped let her know that the goosebumps her breath gave me weren't helping. I rolled my eyes to emphasize my point. She slunk away, presumably to see if she could find any information about the maybe missing girl.

I had to search to find an empty seat to get ready. The spot I had used before was taken by a petite redhead who wore a decidedly unfriendly expression. I didn't dare ask her to move. Her spiked collar and chain bikini made me think we could be friends, but her face said don't even try, so I left her alone and found an empty seat by the bathroom. The two girls nearby were whispering to each other. My first thought was to mind my own business, but what they were saying piqued my interest.

"Did you hear about Taylor?" A perky blonde in a sparkly blue bra said almost under her breath.

"I did, she should have known better though. Talking shit to Angel is always a bad move." The other dancer said, also a blonde, but rail thin.

Their voices got even lower, but I'm almost positive I heard the sparkly blue bra chick say, "She's been taken out I heard."

"Bummer," the thin one said.

My stomach dropped. Could that poor thing really have been killed? No way. But that is what it sounded like. And it seemed like it corresponded to Angel's slightly improved demeanor. I finished getting ready, which didn't take much. I tried to hide my alarm by looking nervous instead. I think it worked because Honey noticed, put her arm around me and whispered some words of encouragement. I checked in with Lars at the DJ booth and scanned the main room for my ghost bestie. She was nowhere to be found. Dom, however, was at the entrance to the VIP room. I walked over to say hello. He flashed a brilliant smile as watched me approach.

"Hello beautiful," he said, and I melted. I nodded awkwardly in return desperately trying to say something that didn't come out awkward.

"Hello yourself," I said awkwardly. I slunk away having failed in my mission.

Colleen didn't show for my first stage. Which explained my lackluster audience. I can't say it did much for my ego or self-esteem to have to acknowledge that she helps so much with the enthusiasm of the customers. But even on my own I didn't do too bad. And having a regular night as opposed to the blockbusters I had on my first two, took some of the heat off me. You didn't have to be a veteran stripper to get that if one girl consistently had every customer, and I mean literally every customer falling over themselves to give them money, the other girls would notice. And not in a positive way. Besides, it's not like they were throwing tomatoes or anything. It was just that I had half the customers paying attention rather than all of them.

Colleen didn't actually show up the whole rest of the night. I did a decent amount of lap dances, but I couldn't stop thinking about where she might have gone off to. And that she was disappearing like this much more often than usual. My thoughts kept straying, making it hard to concentrate on making boners and money. I couldn't help but wonder if she might be losing interest in me. If she had found someone else. Here we are surrounded by sexy women, and it wouldn't be all that hard to see her becoming infatuated with someone else. But I couldn't pull that thread too hard. Thinking about her with someone else dropped my heart into my bowels. By the time the night ended, and Lars was playing the last song, I was getting pretty bummed. The relief I felt when she finally showed up as I was getting dressed to leave made me want to grab and hold her and not let her go. Until she spoke at least.

"Uh, we should get out of here," she said whispering despite the fact that no one else could hear her. I raised my eyebrows in a silent question.

Honey burst through the door and into the dressing room, "There's a dead guy in the VIP!"

14

There weren't that many girls left by that time, most of them having left after their last stages, but the ones that were there gasped in unison. Except for the redhead in chains, she seemed utterly unperturbed. We were all waiting for Honey to elaborate. Her mouth opened to speak, but before she could say anything else, Angel came charging into the room and interrupted. The girls in the room stared at her and held their collective breath. Colleen stuck her tongue out at her. I couldn't help but giggle. Angel still didn't seem to see her.

"A customer has had a medical incident and does not seem to be breathing. We have an ambulance on the way. We can't let anyone leave until they get here." She slinked out the way she came in and everyone let her breath out.

Honey took advantage of the silence, "Ambulance my ass. That guy is fucking dead." She fell into a nearby chair dramatically and threw her head back in a silent scream.

"I think I saw him," a naked blond girl said. "Was he in the back corner booth?"

Honey nodded yes. Even having only been here a short time, I knew what that back corner booth was for. It had been dubbed the naughty booth. The spot where girls who provided a full-service experience for extra tips did their thing. As this booth was conveniently out of view of the cameras.

"I thought he was just having a good time, he looked really surprised," the blond girl said pulling on a pair of jeans.

"I danced for him earlier in the night," Honey said. "In a different booth," she added, her eyebrows scrunched together to make it clear she wasn't 'one of those girls'.

"What was he wearing?" asked the chained-up redhead. It was the first time I had heard her speak. Her voice was like a soft summer rain in direct contradiction to her hard ass look.

"Just jeans and a green polo shirt. Kind of quiet. Nice guy though, I think his name was Paul."

A bell clanged in my head. I remembered dancing for him. And not that long ago. My last dance actually. And it may have been that booth. Not because I was trying to get him off or anything. But because it was the only one available at the time. My stomach turned to stone as I remembered the encounter. We chatted for a few, he was an engineer of some sort, he did seem nice. I did a couple of dances, collected my money and that was it. He had a raging erection, and I left him there to calm down a bit. I guess he's calm enough now.

Colleen wore an expression that I wished at that moment I couldn't read. She knew I had been the last to dance for him. The cement in my stomach liquified and began to slosh around making sickly waves. The back of my throat tightened, and I knew I was about to puke. I fought it back while trying to make my way inconspicuously to the toilet. Suddenly grateful for the undesirable make-up spot by the bathroom. I pulled up the toilet seat in time but splattered the contents of my stomach on the floor anyway.

Colleen's cold hand on the back of my neck shocked my nausea away but not before Honey noticed that I had defiled the small bathroom. Honey stood over me while my head was in the porcelain bowl artfully avoiding the mess on the floor by standing wide legged and straddling it. She had one hand on my back, a warm contrast to my ghost's frigid one.

"It's ok sweetie," she said, her hand rubbing my back. I just nodded my head in agreement afraid to speak and barf again. I was in a bit of a hurry to get my head out of the strip club toilet and didn't want to do anything to disturb the relative calm that had come over my stomach. I started to stand up and Honey backed away. Colleen kept her hand on my neck, her ethereal feet stood in my puke. She wouldn't need to wash it off. Yet another advantage to being dead I suppose.

The three or four girls that were left in the dressing room had all gotten dressed and were looking at me sympathetically. I gave them an embarrassed smile and wiped my mouth with the wad of paper towels that Honey had handed me.

"Sorry," I said to the room.

The redhead, now in her street clothes said, "No worries. The last chick who barfed in here was shitfaced, so at least it wasn't that." The rest of the room nodded in agreement. Nice to be in a place that seemed to hold no judgement. I felt my embarrassment fade slightly, as I heard a siren approach.

"The ambulance is here, this shouldn't take long, and we should be out of here soon," Honey said. It had been obvious from the beginning that she was kind of the mother hen of the club, and that role was on full display right now. All the girls seemed to take comfort in her words. A calm came over the dressing room, and it stayed that way for about ten minutes before Angel came in and decimated it.

"The guy is dead. The paramedics are taking him away. But the police are on their way. It looks like a natural death, but they are going to want statements from the dancers who danced for him."

I felt like puking again.

"It will be fine. You didn't do anything wrong but show the guy a good time. Just tell him the truth and we'll go home to Bert and Ernie. Besides, he's probably in a better place," Colleen said with entirely too much enthusiasm. I rolled my eyes at her which was, unfortunately, in Angel's general direction. My stomach rolled once again as the door twat and possible conspiracy podcaster turned her focus to me. Colleen winced.

"You have something to say Lilith? We're all upset and want to go home," if looks could kill, I'd be as cold and dead as my companion.

"Uh, I know. Sorry I uh…" couldn't finish my sentence. Colleen in her epic wisdom, breezed up Angel's back causing her to inhale sharply at the cold. Effectively distracting her, if only temporarily.

"We've reviewed the cameras, and we need Honey and Lilith to stay as they had the last contact with the customer in question," Angel stared at me while she spoke. The other girls quickly grabbed their stuff and darted out the door. "Wait here," she spat at Honey and me as she too left the room.

Honey had pulled out her phone and was scrolling on it, apparently all out of comforting words. I pulled out my own phone and pretended to be interested in something on the screen. I wasn't. In fact, I spent very little time on my phone at all. Social media was not my thing, and I wasn't into games. But it served as a useful tool to make me look like I was busy. Colleen kind of lurked in the corner along with the smell of puke. I was almost embarrassed again, but anxiety overwhelmed it. Then the cop walked in.

"Hello ladies. I've been told that you two were the last to have contact with the deceased," he was nice looking with his dark hair and porn star mustache. Because of course he was. I hoped he didn't notice the barf and gave him a look that I hoped didn't denote guilt.

"Yes, sir. I danced for him earlier, but Lilith danced for him last," Honey offered unhelpfully.

"Ok, this looks pretty straightforward, and I just need a quick statement from you, and I'll be on my way," the cop said. He turned to Honey, "Can you step out into the hallway with me?" She nodded and followed him out of the dressing room out of earshot.

"What the fuck?" I whispered to Colleen.

"It will be fine. I'm sure this kind of stuff happens all the time." I doubted that and rolled my eyes at her. And this time no one else saw. She shrugged. "Like I said, just tell him the truth. No big deal."

I sat there amid the glitter and puke wishing Dom were here. And then wished again that he were here, but without the puke. I pictured us instead at a nice restaurant, sitting across from his broad shoulders and devastating smile. Talking and flirting over candlelight.

My eyes were closed when the cop came back into the room, and I realized I had been wearing a bit of a smile. My eyes shot open, and I put an appropriately somber expression on my face. The last thing I needed was this cop seeing me smile.

"Hello, I'm sorry. I'll make this quick. It's really just a formality," the tall dark and handsome cop said. His name badge read 'Smith'. Officer Smith was cute, my eyes drifted to his handcuffs. He noticed, and I think he may have smirked. "Can you tell me about what time you first talked to the deceased?" His eyes were kind, but any trace of a smirk was gone.

"Uh, I wasn't wearing a watch," I giggled, totally inappropriately. But in my defense the question was kind of silly, as I hadn't been wearing anything but a G-string and a pair of fuck-me pumps. Colleen looked at me with wide eyes, telling me to cool it. Easy for her to say. She didn't kill the dude. "I think it must have been around two. I asked him for a lap dance, and we went to the VIP room. We chatted for a few minutes, and I danced for, I think, two...no, three songs. And then I left. He seemed fine." I was rambling.

"No heavy breathing, or sweating..."

"Well...yeah," I giggled again. I wasn't doing myself any favors. I really needed to stop having reasons to talk to cops.

"Dude. Hold it together," Colleen whispered.

"I'm sorry, I'm just so tired and a little nervous," I said.

"That's understandable. Doesn't help that it stinks in here." I nodded in agreement, hoping that it didn't infer my culpability for the barf. "Like I said, just a formality. I've heard about this kind of thing before. Guy gets worked up, blows a fuse and that's it. But you didn't notice anything out of the ordinary? Did he smell like booze, maybe seem like he was on drugs?"

"I really don't think so. I haven't been doing this for very long. But it all seemed normal, or as normal as it gets in the strip club." It was the cop's turn to nod in agreement. I felt a little better, and as a bonus I don't think he blamed me for the smell.

The good-looking cop took my real name and contact information and said goodbye. I looked at the tired clock on the wall and saw that the sun would be up soon. I grabbed my stuff and began to walk out of the dressing room. I had my head down and didn't see Dom walking in. I bumped into him. The soapy water in the mop bucket he was carrying sloshed and splashed my shoes.

"Oh, I'm so sorry," I said. Embarrassment rising to the surface again.

"No worries little lady, everyone gets a little sick from time to time," and I wanted to die.

15

The darkness was fading as I pushed open the front door of the club. The sun was coming up and all I wanted to do was lie down. My brain was fried, and my stomach felt like it was full of sand. Since all the customers were long gone, and Dom was busy cleaning up the remains of my dinner from the night before, I had walked out to my car alone. Well not quite. Colleen was with me.

The ambulance and Paul's corpse were gone too. The cop hadn't hung around to put up any crime tape, so I had good reason to think there wouldn't be any investigation. Probably just an autopsy that would reveal some sort of heart condition or an overdose of cocaine. But I leaned toward heart attack, given Honey's melodramatic depiction of his body. Like Colleen said, it didn't seem to be a deal after all. Besides, he really seemed totally normal. I think I would have known if he was high. The interior temperature of my car dropped as Colleen slid through the passenger door and into the seat.

"What a night, I feel really bad for that guy. I hope it wasn't my fault," I said to her.

"I don't think your lap dances are that good."

"Gee thanks," I rolled my eyes yet again.

"Meh, people die suddenly all the time," she said. "Haven't you seen that viral video? It's all the vaccines."

"Wait. I thought the vaccines were a delivery system for the mind control microchips activated by the 5G cell towers?"

"That was a different video. Try and keep up," I rolled my eyes again. At this rate I'll be the only stripper saving up for new eyeballs instead of boobs. But for just a split second I wondered if she wasn't just joking about all this stuff.

"My bad. Where were you all night?"

"I was poking around. I saw no sign of Taylor. But I heard Pete the bartender say he was going to miss her."

"She could have left and gone somewhere else. Just because she wasn't there doesn't mean she's dead." I wondered if I was trying to convince myself that something bad hadn't happened to the girl. There weren't any other clubs in the area, so it didn't seem likely that she had gone to work anywhere else. Unless she just moved out of the area.

"Really? Even after hearing her podcast? You aren't suspicious?" Colleen looked at me with raised eyebrows.

"I guess a little. But the whole cult murder thing seems pretty far-fetched. If I wanted to go down that road, I might think that she was responsible for this guy's death too."

"Far-fetched, you're talking to a ghost for fuck's sake."

"Fair point. And I guess she could have slipped him some poison or something. But why?"

"Well, narcissistic cult leaders do shit just to feed their egos. That definitely seems consistent with Angel's personality. Drum up some drama, gain support. Do your research. It's all par for the course with people like her."

Colleen was making sense, but I still couldn't shake the feeling like she wasn't telling me everything. Or maybe she was really starting to buy into all the junk she finds online. I couldn't think of a reason she would lie to me. But everything was pointing to Angel. Her attitude, the way the staff kissed her wrinkly butt was suspect for sure. I don't actually know if her butt is wrinkly or not by the way, but it is in my imagination. Not to mention the way the girls seemed to be afraid of her, you didn't have to have much interaction with her to know that something was seriously off. Or to know that she had a certain hold over the people at the club. Online cult leader didn't seem so far off if I took all those things into consideration. All these thoughts were swimming around my exhausted brain, and it seemed best not to try to overthink it all until I could get some rest.

I wished I had sunglasses as I finished the drive home. The sun was becoming aggressive, and the drive seemed endless. The sight of my driveway was just about the most beautiful thing I had ever seen. I dragged myself out of my car and into my house. Richard was waiting and looking worried as I walked in. Then he saw Colleen and looked pissed. He hissed at her but held his position on the edge of the sofa. I picked him up and nuzzled him under my chin. I walked him into my bedroom and deposited him on the bed. I closed the curtains and stripped. I didn't even bother to brush my teeth. All I wanted at that moment was to crawl under the covers and into the land of the unconscious. Colleen kissed me on the cheek, and I drifted off.

A heavy metal guitar riff woke me around 6 hours later. My ringtone. My room was dark thanks to my heavy bedroom curtains. Colleen was lying next to me. I rolled over to look at my phone. It was the club calling. I was about to answer it, but it must have been ringing for a while because when I pressed the green button the call had already gone to voicemail. I played the message on speaker. It was Rick. He was asking if I would come in for the night shift. I wasn't scheduled, but he said that a bunch of girls had called out. He didn't say why, but I guessed it had something to do with the dead guy the night before. I rolled over and considered the offer. I didn't need the money. Not at all. I had plenty of cash stacked up. Becoming a stripper was the best financial decision I had ever made. But that made me think that I should go in. The last thing I wanted to do was look for another job. And I didn't know of any more elderly ladies hoarding cash next to their Nazi memorabilia.

"Are you going to go in?" Colleen asked.

"I guess I should," I replied. I had a few hours before the night shift started. I was starving and in dire need of coffee. Colleen read my mind. She blew into the kitchen and started the coffee maker. I sent a text to the number Rick had called from, telling him that I would be in. He responded immediately with a "thanks" and a smiley face emoji.

I was still thinking about the events of the night before. I felt bad about Paul but didn't feel guilty any longer. Although, I did hope that it was just a random heart attack and nothing more sinister. Despite my having just started, it isn't inconceivable that my lap dance was actually good enough to induce sudden heart failure. I almost always get a standing ovation. That means an erection in stripper lingo. Even if she did kill Taylor, I didn't see a reason to believe that Angel had killed the customer just for kicks. Cuntface or not.

Colleen had brought in the laptop with our coffee and had pulled up the Dark Angel podcast. We sipped as she played the latest episode. That strange voice that had at first listen sounded androgenous, now took on a more female quality. And dare I say, even started to resemble the Embers Gentleman's Club door girl.

"Loyal listeners, I need your help. As you need mine. You have been drawn to me in your time of need, as fate intended. Last night, I received a message from our divine creator. My loves, the evil cabal is trying to thwart our goodness. They are trying to subvert our very souls. They are the voices that disparage my character. They say that I am the threat. They want your demise and mine. Without your undying love, they will win. Thanks to your contributions and sacrifices, I have been able to remove an enemy that came very close to destroying me. There was another who was taken as well, and while taking of life is not easy, our creator is never wrong. As always it came in the form of innocence and beauty. Evil is never ugly. It is young and pretty and feigns naivete. It disarms as it captivates. I fear for you, my loves. Far more than I fear for myself. I fear the persecution that we face as we try to right the wrongs of this world and collect our reward in the next one. That is why you were drawn to me. Because you are special, you are loved. And together we will prevail. But not without protection. And I, your chosen divine prophet, have provided that protection. If this world were not so evil, I would send each of you one of my protection amulets without cost. But fighting evil is not free. And we must play the game according to the rules that are set out. And your love, and support is how I was able to stop that beautiful creature from derailing our plans and damning us to the eternal underworld that is trying to suck us down."

I looked at Colleen, who was listening as intently as I was.

"Did you hear that? There was another taken? I think she might be responsible for both Taylor and that customer. What do we do? We don't have anything to take to the police except this podcast."

I could hardly believe what I was saying, but all this couldn't be a coincidence. And the last damn thing I needed was another encounter with any kind of law enforcement.

"I'm a ghost, not a nutter. Angel isn't just a huge cunt, she's a murderer. We have to stop her."

Colleen was right. I hopped out of bed and started to get ready for work. I didn't have any idea how we would find the evidence to stop Angel, but we had to try.

16

Colleen

Paul was an accident. My bad. Lacey's dance was good enough to get him going, but not that good. And he wasn't coked up, but he did have a few drinks in him. His buzz had him just sleepy enough to start to drift off. He sat there after she left and closed his eyes, and I well… I got what I needed from him. Seriously, I did *not* mean to kill him. Total accident. I didn't even know it was happening until I finished and looked at him. The poor guy, face frozen like that. Like he had leg cramp while jerking off. I guess that's kind of what happened. Just a tad more severe.

I also didn't mean to make Lacey think that Angel had killed him along with that dancer. She followed that carrot down the rabbit hole on her own. Once again, not my fault. But it's not like I can tell her what really happened. That would open up a whole other conversation I'm not ready to have. In essence it's not really lying. Just a series of unfortunate accidents. All not intended, but simply a consequence of my very existence. And one I'm determined to overcome. People change, why not demons?

Besides Angel is the real evil being here. She must be behind that podcast. Taylor is gone. I'm sure I would have heard the staff and such talking about where she went if she weren't dead. Instead of that they were just going to miss her. Granted I spent most of the night lingering around the VIP room. Kind of an irresistible place for a demon like me. The sexually charged atmosphere is kind of my jam. I wasn't even planning on getting anything. Until I just couldn't help myself anymore.

Lacey doesn't know that I can make myself invisible to her and not just other people. But once again, not a liar. I just wouldn't want to upset what we have going on here. I wouldn't know what to do without her. Shit, I don't even know what I did do without her. For all I know, she could be the reason I exist. I don't want to fuck it up. I tell her all the important things. That's what matters.

Besides, we know that Angel killed Taylor and that's enough reason to figure out how to stop her. An extra corpse pinned on her might even make it easier for the cops to get her anyway. And it's not like I did it on purpose. Really, Paul might end up helping us put a stop to Angel and her grift. You might even say Paul's accidental death was a good thing. Think of all the people we'll save when we get her. Not to mention all the people who have bought her online crap. I'm a helper.

17

The club looked to be pretty dead when I walked in on Sunday evening. There wasn't much going on at all. Only a few customers dotted the main floor. I wondered if word of the dead guy in the VIP had gotten out to the public. But I didn't think so. It didn't make the news, I checked. The dressing room was just as dead.

I had braced myself for Angel's sneers when I walked in but was instead greeted by another door girl. Jess was her name. She worked Sundays and Mondays when Angel was off. She said hello with a warm smile, and I was stunned when she didn't insult me in a backhanded creepy way. I almost didn't know how to react. But Colleen did. She poked me in the back after the awkward silence I had created became untenable. I smiled back, said hello, and dropped a five in her tip jar.

I had my pick of spots to get ready because there were only two other girls in the dressing room. Lexus and Jasmine were talking in not quite whispers which stopped abruptly when I walked in.

"Hey girl!" Lexus said, topless. I was accustomed to being around nudity, but I couldn't help staring at her ample boobs. They were kind of hard to miss. Jasmine gave me a quick head nod, which I returned.

"Hey."

"Did you hear about the guy that died last night?"

"Well, yeah. I was here. Just a heart attack, but pretty upsetting," Lexus looked unimpressed with my answer.

"Huh, just a heart attack. That sucks," she said. I wondered just how much the girls and staff knew about Angel and her following. They were afraid of upsetting her, that was easy to see. But did they know about the podcast and all that too?

"Angel came in at the end of the night and told us that a guy had had a medical issue and that an ambulance was on the way. They couldn't revive him, and a cop came and talked to a couple of girls who had danced for him. It was a bummer, but it didn't seem like that much of a big deal."

"I heard that one of the girls was so upset that they threw up," Lexus cringed. Jasmine stayed quiet but wrinkled her nose.

"Yeah, I heard that too. I mean it was a dead guy, I'm sure it's natural for someone to be upset." Colleen looked at me and shrugged.

"I bet you didn't have time to be upset. You've really been busy," Jasmine broke her silence and looked to instantly regret it.

"Yeah, just beginner's luck I think," I said, and both girls looked at each other. Mentioning the door girl's name almost seemed taboo, but with her off that night I felt like this was the best time to gather some information. "Angel seemed really cool about it. Is that something that has happened before?"

"No. Not that I've ever heard of. And that's just how she is. She handles the books and is very close to the owner. She was one of the first girls to work here when it opened. She's an OG," Lexus said. "The owner is here today, by the way. So is Angel. They're upstairs. Beginner's luck has certainly been kind to you. Guys seem to be really happy with your performances," her eyes narrowed. I understood that she and Jasmine were insinuating that I was doing favors in the naughty booth. Given that the last guy died there, and I was the last to dance for him, I could see why they would think that.

"I'm just doing what I've seen the other girls do," I said, way too defensively. "Last night was really busy. I think everyone was having a really good night. At least until…"

"Yeah, I heard you've really been killing it," Jasmine said, making me like her better when she was quiet. Colleen of course was giggling in the corner.

"We heard that you and Honey danced for the dead guy," Lexus said. She still had her top off and her boobs jiggled hypnotically as she spoke. I managed to keep eye contact though. "Hey precious, my boobs are down here." Lexus bounced up and down, her breasts wobbled like unrestrained jello. I started to laugh, but then remembered her question and stopped abruptly. She was thinking that not only was I doing special favors but that I killed that guy too? I didn't know how to stop this conversation from getting worse.

"I did. I think I was the last one too. I had to talk to the cop. But he didn't seem all that concerned. Said that guys had heart attacks all the time during lap dances."

Both strippers looked skeptical at that.

"I've never heard of a customer dying of a heart attack like that. And I've been dancing a long…long time," Jasmine said, with exactly no humor in her voice.

"Yeah, it does sound a little sketchy," Lexus said, her humor had also deserted her. I think I saw her eyes narrow just a tiny bit. "I doubt your lap dances are *that* good, but it must be weird to have danced for a dude right before he died."

"She's just jealous and trying to fuck with you," Colleen said.

"It *was* weird. Honestly freaked me out a little bit. Well, freaked me out a lot. I'd really like to try and forget about it if I could." I could feel the frown on my face.

"Hey, are you the one that barfed?" Lexus said, and the last bit of fondness I thought I had for her drained away. "I'd barf too if I had to talk to a cop after a guy I had danced for dropped dead." Her boobs had suddenly lost their appeal too.

"Uh, I think I ate something bad," I said like a complete idiot. And to think I could have totally stayed home.

My last statement lingered in the air of the dressing room like the odor from a bag of burned popcorn, while I got ready. I did it as quickly as I could and checked in at the DJ booth. A very large man, who was not Lars was working the sound system.

"I'm Ernie," he said. And Colleen snickered behind me, as a smile crept to my face, and I suppressed a giggle. Ernie looked at me with his eyebrows drawn together. "I say something funny?"

"Oh no, it's just your name," I blurted. "I mean something funny about your name." I really just shouldn't be allowed to talk to anyone. Ever. Ernie didn't look amused.

"Dude shut up. I can't take you anywhere," Colleen said. Still snickering.

"I'm so sorry. Inside joke." Ugh, that didn't help. Inside joke with who? My whispering ghost? He was almost sneering at me now. "I'm Lilith." I smiled, but his sneer wasn't affected.

"You got a few more songs before you're up. Lars left me a file with some of your songs. We don't have a lot of girls, and I can't guarantee that I can skip you if you're in the VIP. So don't expect to miss any stages." He said and turned back toward the equipment, an obvious indication that our conversation was over. There were other staff in the club that I hadn't met. The bartender was a skinny little blond dude, who seemed painfully quiet, and a squat bald bouncer, whose face was glued to the screen of his phone. The only staff member I knew besides the two girls was Rick the Manager.

The main room of the club was empty except for two dilapidated gentlemen in nearly identical trench coats. I wondered if there was a special shop that catered specifically to dirty old men and noir styled PIs. Not having anyone to talk to, and not wanting to go back into the dressing room, I approached one of them. He was sitting in a dark corner at the very back of the room. Literally the farthest away he could be from the stage and still be in the club. The closer I got, the more I questioned my decision to talk to him.

"Oooo, you should skip this one," Colleen said behind me. Tragically much too late as I had already made eye contact with the guy. The odor of booze and piss smacked me upside the head, as I got within speaking distance.

"Oh, hello," I paused, and then said brilliantly, "I'm sorry, I thought you were someone else. Have a good night." I smiled brightly and turned to walk away. This guy and his stench weren't going to let me off that easily.

"Hi, little lady. Are you sure you aren't available to sit for a few minutes. I can't imagine where you would be getting off to. There's no one here." He laughed heartily before erupting into a coughing fit.

"Uh, I got to go." I glanced behind me to look at Colleen, hoping she wasn't charming this guy into liking me. But she shrugged her shoulders. His coughing fit ended, and he smiled a huge goofy grin. The smell was making my eyes water, but he didn't seem like he was altogether a bad dude. "I guess I have just a few minutes." I took a seat as far away as I could get from him while still being able to talk to him. He handed me a five-dollar bill with that same grin on his face.

"Here's a little something for you," he said. And then began to talk. And talk. And talk. If I had a gun to my head, I wouldn't be able to tell what he talked about. Not even his name. When Ernie finally called my name, I felt like I had been sitting there for hours, but it had only been a few songs.

My reprieve only lasted so long, however. When I got down from the stage, he was waiting for me. I was about to tell him that I couldn't sit with him, but Rick saw me and called me over to where he was at the bar. As I was walking over to him, I saw Angel walking through the floor wearing a huge smile and talking to a short guy wearing a buzz cut and a blue track suit. He was matching her smile. She must have said something funny, because he began to laugh and threw his arm around her shoulders. They walked that way all the way to the front door.

Rick didn't bother saying hello as I got within earshot of him, "I see that Claude has taken a liking to you. He does that with the new girls. He is a long-time customer and important to the owner. I know it sucks, but you must sit with him if he asks. He'll complain to the staff if you don't. He is only here on Sundays and as soon as we get another new girl, he'll forget about you. Sorry. But that is the deal."

I could feel Colleen behind me shaking her head. I just nodded to Rick. As I walked back to the smiling Claude, I whispered to Colleen, "Is there anything you can do?"

"I'm so sorry, but I can only nudge a little. I'll make him really cold, and maybe he'll just leave."

And so went the rest of my night. Stages, and Claude, stages, and Claude. Colleen's chill did nothing but make him complain about how bad the chill was that night. It was the first time I had started to rethink my job. But at least Colleen stayed next to me the whole time, so I didn't have to suffer alone. By the time the last song had played, I couldn't get to the dressing room fast enough.

Lexus was already dressed when I opened the door, "Hey, I saw you got stuck with Claude all night. Tough break."

"Not the best night I've had," I said, kicking off my shoes.

"But hey, once he hears that the last guy you danced for croaked, I bet he'll move on."

15

To add to the worst night I've had so far as a stripper, Dom wasn't there to walk me out. Not that I had a problem with the guy who did, it just wasn't Dom. But maybe that wasn't such a bad thing, given our last exchange was when he was going to clean up my barf. I was really hoping that he might forget about it by the time I saw him again. Other than his ridiculously good looks I'm not even sure why I liked him so much. I don't know much about him. He could be a real dick, just a really handsome one. Although, Lexus was good looking too, and I didn't like her at all.

"So, what the actual fuck is up with Lexus?" I asked my chilly friend.

"Don't trip chocolate chip," she replied. "She's just jealous. You put a bunch of chicks together with latent insecurities and have them all compete with their looks for their rent, and you're bound to have some haters."

I had to admit she had a point. Although, seeing as that I had made pretty much no money because I had to sit with old smelly all night, it was hard to see how she could be jealous of that. But Colleen was likely right, sometimes mean girls are just mean because of course they are. It didn't take very long to notice the middle school-esque type politics at the club. This girl danced to this other girl's song without asking. Or that girl talked to another girl's regular. The type of petty bullshit that is pretty much the reason I avoid most people in the first place. It had only been a week, but it wasn't hard to figure out that the best position to take when hearing gossip was no position at all. Just call me Switzerland, neutral as fuck.

"That makes sense, I guess. I just wish she had picked a different way to fuck with me. Like she couldn't have made fun of my hair or boobs or something."

"You know, how about we get out of town. Maybe take a little trip or something. Take a break from all this bullshit. We have definitely earned it," my ghost deftly changed the subject. Which was fabulous, because I was ready to be done talking about the club and everyone in it.

"That sounds like a fine plan."

We drove in silence until we got back to the house. Richard was waiting in the dark, perched on the edge of the sofa as we walked in. He meowed at me, a request for food more likely than a loving greeting. But he refrained from hissing or growling at Colleen. A notable improvement in their strained relationship. I patted him on the head to show my approval. My work bag landed with a thump as I dropped it on the floor and promptly went into the kitchen to fill his dish. With my furry buddy fed, I nuked a frozen burrito for myself and stuffed it in my mouth while my ghost buddy watched and smiled.

"How about going into the country? Maybe take a little hike, find a bed and breakfast?" I asked Colleen. I didn't really have anyone to take care of Richard, so I didn't think I wanted to be gone more than one night. He would be pissed enough off at that.

"That sounds perfect. Dick will hate you."

"Well, of course. But he might appreciate not having to look at your ugly mug for a night." She grabbed me and planted a cool kiss on my cheek which currently held a large bite of microwave burrito.

"As long as you still like me, I'm not worried about that little dick."

One of the best things about a ghost lover is that she doesn't seem to give a shit about burrito breath. Or at least Colleen gave no indication that she did as she pulled me into our room and into our bed. She worked her magic, and soon I was fast asleep.

I awoke warm, but not alone. I was snuggled in the embrace of a man. The scent of sandalwood and cedar filled my senses as I breathed. My head was nestled on the chest of Dom with my shoulder in crook of his arm, as he held me. He kissed the top of my head and cooed. "Good morning my love."

I smiled and buried myself deeper in the cozy embrace before panic brought me awake for real. A strange sense of guilt, or maybe just disloyalty flooded my body and jolted me upright. The dream of the dreamy bouncer started to fade as I realized that I was alone. Well except for Richard, who was curled up on Colleen's vacant pillow.

I smelled coffee in the air and heard Colleen in the living room tapping away at the keyboard of the computer. I hoped she was perusing a flat earth website and not searching for more information on our shared nemesis and conspiracy podcaster. While I knew that the drama with the salty door girl was far from over, I just wanted a break. Even a small reprieve from having to think about her and the club would do me good. Maybe some distance would offer a more objective view of the situation.

I scratched Richard between the ears and planted a small kiss on the top of his head. He was lost in cat dream land but purred anyway. I slipped out of bed and into the living room where Colleen was sitting on the sofa.

"Good morning, Sunshine!" I belted. She jumped and toppled the computer onto the floor. "Careful, a new computer is like fifteen lap dances."

"You scared me," she giggled. "Impressive, you scared a ghost."

I kissed her cheek. She bent down and picked up the laptop. I could see that she had been looking at places to stay in the country. Relieved, I kissed her again but on the mouth. I stopped her when her hand moved to my boob, stiffening my nipple.

"Nope, coffee first." I dashed into the kitchen to grab two mugs.

When I got back, Colleen had moved to the dining room table. She took a sip of her coffee and showed me what she had found. It was a little place in a town I had been to with my mother as a kid. In the foothills of the Sierra Mountains, this little town had been part of the gold rush in the 1860's. It was now a tourist attraction that didn't get all that many tourists. I remembered that there was a small museum and one of the old houses had been turned into an ice cream shop. My mom had taken me there after the museum for ice cream. It was just after my dad passed. Colleen noticed the tears in my eyes and put her arm around me. I leaned into her for a moment, grateful I wasn't alone.

"I went here with my mom when I was little."

"We can find someplace else. There's a ton. It's a big state."

"No. I think this town is perfect. It's a tad creepy, and full of ghost stories. Maybe you'll run into someone you know?" I winked, but she didn't seem to notice.

"There are some trails nearby, and here is where I thought we could stay."

She clicked and a Victorian style house filled the screen. The three-story lavender house had white trim. Dark green ivy crawled up the pillars that framed the porch and led to the front door. It looked new but had to be very old. It advertised soft beds and a full-service breakfast served at the very reasonable time of ten am. It was located on the main street of the town and there were several restaurants and shops close by. It was just the thing we needed to forget about everything for a while.

"Let's book it," I said.

I called the number and made reservations for the next day, checking to make sure they took cash. When it was done, I commandeered the computer and poked around to find more information on the little gold rush town. I couldn't escape the sense of melancholy I felt as the memory of my mom bloomed in my mind. I had been so wrapped up with Colleen that I realized I hadn't thought of her in some time. I hoped she was in a better place, as Colleen was apt to say. But I wondered if she really knew or not.

I found a couple of trails, that even on the weekend wouldn't be crowded. We were going to go during the middle of the week, so I figured they would be deserted. I closed the computer, and turned to my companion, who was looking at me under her eyelashes. No wonder I had no time to think about anything else.

"So naked pizza and Netflix?" She wore an evil smile.

"Hell yes."

16

The next morning Colleen woke me up at 9am, an ungodly hour if there ever was one. She kissed my forehead and yanked me out of a dream that I thought I was really enjoying but instantly evaporated when my eyes opened. We had fallen asleep early at least, and she had my favorite mug filled with coffee for me in her hand. Richard, who had been sleeping at the foot of the bed, was not pleased to be woken up either. He gave a dirty look to rival Angel's and went back to sleep with a grunt.

"Are you ready?" She sat on the edge of the bed waiting for me to sit up so she could hand me my mug.

"You obviously are, me not so much," I took a long drink of my coffee. It was hot, strong and delicious. Dom floated into my mind for some silly reason. "Ok, let me go get in the shower and we'll get moving." I set my mug down to get out of bed but promptly picked it up again to bring it with me into the bathroom.

"You know it might go faster if I come with you."

"I actually think that will take longer, but if you insist."

The hot water steamed off of her as she stepped in with me. And like I thought, it did take just a little longer than it would have had I showered alone. But I have no regrets.

We got out and toweled off. Colleen was gathering some stuff to take with us. She packed up some pot and put the computer in its travel case, but I stopped her.

"Please, can we leave that here?" She pouted but put it back on the table. I packed an overnight bag, and filled two dishes with food for Richard, who so far hadn't noticed that anything was amiss. I locked up the house and we headed out to the car.

The road was full of twists and turns as we drove up the hill. My small compact car took the turns pretty well. We passed a lot of big rigs hauling the remains of majestic oak trees on the other side of the road. We screamed along to heavy metal songs until we reached the sleepy little town. I was delighted to see that it was almost deserted. The last thing I wanted was to be around a bunch of people.

As we pulled onto the main street of town, I saw a couple of dudes in dirty jeans and t-shirts, both wearing beards that hung down to their chests. They eyed my car suspiciously as I drove down the street. The town didn't look quite like it did on the internet. Other than a few signs marking what must have been historical sites, it didn't have the touristy feel that it had promised online. I felt a bit like an interloper. And the two guys were peering into my car as if I shouldn't be there, weren't helping. In my head, a banjo twanged ominously.

"Hey, so what do you think about going solid while we're here? I'm not sure it's a great idea if people think I'm alone." Given Colleen's propensity to make me giggle inappropriately, the last thing I wanted to do was look like I was laughing to myself. This place being surrounded by desolate woods and all.

"Are you sure? I think sometimes I look a little weird to people." She was wearing the haggard Iron Maiden shirt I met her in and her torn jeans. I wasn't sure if I should tell her that at least here, she probably wouldn't look that weird.

"Meh, you look perfect. And we can have a proper dinner together." I glanced around again and noticed a small, but still noticeable confederate flag in the window of the sundry shop. "Might be a good idea if we don't make out or hold hands or anything." She seemed a little perplexed at that. I'm not sure if she was picking up what I was putting down, but I didn't really want to elaborate. Although, two chicks were usually easier to take than two dudes, if this town bore the kind of attitude that I suspected it did. I wasn't looking for any kind of trouble. Nor did I have any desire to help foster any of these guys' fantasies. I did that at work, and I was on vacation.

This was the kind of thing that made me wish I knew more about her life. Colleen had sweet naivete about her, that made me think she must have been very sheltered. But in a hypersexual way. She seemed to know so little of the world, which was charming, but also perplexing. Her raw curiosity and utter lust for life were hard not to love but left a lot of unanswered questions. Like how she could be so oblivious to people and their prejudices. But I supposed it was because she was from another time.

"Ok, I'll save it for when we get to the room. Bert and Ernie may have snuck into your bag." She winked, and I noticed that she had gone solid. I cringed a little on the inside, hoping that *Jethro* and *Cletus* hadn't seen an eighties rocker chick suddenly appear in my passenger seat.

The bed and breakfast was located at the end of the main street and was just as advertised. Even if the town wasn't. The old, converted house looked just like the pictures. I'm not sure if I've ever seen a more beautiful home. The plaque at the bottom of the steps told us that it was built during the gold rush as a hotel for the miners. At least the successful ones. It had spent some time as a single-family residence for one of the business owners that sold mining supplies. I remember learning as a kid that it wasn't the gold seekers that got rich, but the shop, bar, and brothel owners. The majority of the gold miners ended up broke and destitute. Go figure.

I started to get nervous as we walked up the stairs. The new paint didn't do much to hide their age as they creaked when we climbed them. Kind of like Angel's pancake make-up. The front door was in the same condition. I felt even more like an interloper when I turned the knob and pushed open the door. Like I was sneaking into some old lady's house. Something I would never do. Well… almost never. Maybe just something I might do once. Colleen was right behind me, her excited chill had me a little on edge. Which is probably why I nearly screamed when the bell tinkled as the door brushed against it.

We stepped back in time. Sort of. More like the floral section of a craft store. Flowers both real and imagined covered the entire space. Wallpaper, upholstery, even the rug. Excessive, but it really set the grandma's house ambience. An older lady appeared behind the dark wood counter wearing a floral dress. I'm not sure where she had come from actually. One second the counter was empty and the next, there she was. I had to wonder if she was a ghost. I looked over to Colleen to see if she had noticed. She didn't. According to the internet, this place was full of ghosts. And not just this place, but the whole town.

"Can I help you?" the flowered lady said, "I'm Margaret, the Innkeeper." She didn't appear to be looking at us funny, although maybe she was just good at hiding it. We probably did look a little funny. Two chicks, one ridiculously good looking in old clothes, and the other dressed in black with turquoise streaks in her hair. I told her how she could help and after a few minutes, she did.

She gave us an old-fashioned brass key and directed us to our room.

We climbed up the creaky but carpeted stairs and into one of the rooms that we had seen on the website which had a slightly less floral theme than the rest of the building. Margaret had told us that we were the only guests that night. I was not disappointed at that news at all. This was the first time that I had ever really been in public with Colleen pretending to be a live person, and I didn't want to draw too much attention. There's nothing like the first week working at a strip club to make you not want to hang around a bunch of people too.

We tossed our stuff down on one of the two double beds. It was early afternoon, and we had the whole night and place to ourselves. Colleen bounced on the other bed, as I unpacked a few things. Bert and Ernie were indeed in my bag, I took them out and put them on the bed along with some bathroom stuff. Colleen stopped bouncing at looked at me.

"Poor thing. I bet they're restless from riding in the car. We should give them some exercise," she winked again, and I rolled my eyes. But of course, I gave in. Who knew ghosts were so damned horny?

On the nightstand, the old timey rotary phone rang. It scared me so much that I nearly screamed. Although I had been kind of screaming already. It was Margaret. Complaining about the noise. I apologized and hung up. Colleen and I shared a smirk and kept going.

17

I had wrongly assumed that the proprietor of this establishment was hard of hearing. But at least she didn't kick us out. Being the only guests probably helped too.

After I caught my breath, I opened up one of the brochures that we had picked up along with a very nice tote bag with a picture of the bed and breakfast on it as we checked in. The brochure showed a short walking trail that featured some of the old buildings, a cemetery and the small museum that were in the area. We put our clothes back on and crept out the front door, successfully avoiding the annoyed Innkeeper.

The warmth of the country sun as we stepped out of the now even more haunted bed and breakfast felt wonderful. Colleen turned her pale face to the sky, and I wondered if she would need sunscreen. Do ghosts get sunburned? I didn't think much about the logistics of such things when we were alone.

"Oh wow, this feels great," she said with that childlike wonder I found so endearing. If someone had told me that I would someday fall in love with a dead person, a dead woman, I would have happily told them to go fuck themselves and to seek professional help.

"It is nice. Let's go check out some history," I said. I could hardly wait to get to the cemetery. Although it made me feel like kind of a dick. I was horribly curious to see if she would see or sense any other spirits. She picked this place after all. Since she came into my life, I don't think we have been in any place that I would have thought was haunted. Although to be fair, I didn't believe in ghosts until I met Colleen. The dead guy in the VIP bothered me, and not just because he died right after I danced for him. But because he had made me think. If Colleen was a ghost, it seemed reasonable that she would be able to see other ghosts. Wouldn't she have seen the VIP guy Paul's ghost? Or Mary's? Or Taylor's for that matter. If she could see ghosts, this would be the place to see one.

It was a short walk to the trail head. We passed a small bar that looked to only serve tourists out of obligation. I took note though. I hadn't had any real interaction with a guy since I acquired that T-shirt from what's his name. Scott, I think. Colleen was solid, and what better way to forget about stuff than a ménage à trois?

We walked through town before we started on the deserted trail, and it wasn't long before we came to the small mining cabin. It was locked up tight, but the windows were all clear and the inside was set up to look like it might have when someone had lived there. A wooden bed sat near a wood stove, and my back hurt just looking at it. I kept an eye on Colleen, and she was enthralled with the small building. But nothing else.

Colleen and I strolled under a canopy of trees down the dirt trail, in a place that should be, or was at least reported to be one of the most haunted places in the country. There was plenty to be distracted by. The flowers and the squirrels dominated her attention. While we didn't live in the city, but a suburb, this place made our home feel like it was in the middle of a metropolis. There were no sounds except our footfalls and the birds rustling the leaves overhead. I let the small bit of conversation that we had fade, as I looked for any evidence of another being like my best friend. I did not expect to see a ghost other than Colleen. But I did expect her to. Unless it could be that ghosts couldn't see other ghosts, but that didn't seem to make sense. I kept stealing glances her way, waiting for some reaction or any indication that she saw a spirit. My efforts were only rewarded with more of the innocent inquisitiveness with which she approached the world. I loved her but was becoming suspicious of her true origins. Was this beautiful creature what she said she was?

We came to the old and possibly deliberately decrepit cemetery, where there were entirely too many young graves. It was the last stop on the trail before the museum. The crumbling headstones almost looked too creepy to have happened organically. They looked staged. The largest part of the marking plan for the town and the hotel were the tales of hauntings by jilted lovers, failed miners, and almost comically horrific accidental deaths. Including one harrowing tale of a poor man who had acquired syphilis from a local prostitute. When the infection started to take over his brain, his wife, probably out of spite, chained him to the cellar wall where he apparently screamed obscenities until he died. Visitors reported hearing sounds of rattling chains and groans coming from the damp cellar. And yet, Colleen walked among the graves utterly unperturbed. There was a moment where I thought she may have noticed me looking at her, but nothing. The ghost hunters with their equipment seemed to have no problem documenting *evidence* of spirits. I read a few of their blogs. But here I was with an actual ghost, and she saw nothing. The irony was becoming too much, but I held my tongue.

We finally came to the small museum, which was the newest building we had seen since pulling into town. It gave us a more in-depth, but far less sensational, history of the area. There was no mention of the ghost sightings or supernatural rumors that littered the ads for the place. They lured people in with provocative tales of death and evidence of the afterlife, then smacked them in the face with the real historical facts. Quite the clever bait and switch if you ask me. We came to a section that talked about all the child graves in the old cemetery. It mentioned that before the widespread use of vaccines, it was kind of a crapshoot whether your kid would make it to adulthood or not. Up until then, there had been a kind of pregnant silence between us. It was becoming borderline awkward. At least until I opened my mouth and pushed it over the edge.

"I bet that part was paid for by big Pharma," I said. Colleen looked alarmed and shook her head. A reaction that struck me as totally weird until I saw that a docent had heard me and didn't get the joke. "I mean, that sucks about all the dead kids, and I don't even like kids." I added, making it much, much worse. It's a gift.

It was close to dinner time, so we thought it would be a good time to bail. I dropped a ten in the donation box as Colleen beamed a smile at the frowning docent on our way out the door. We made our way back to the main street and into a small country café that advertised the best Country Fried Steak in the whole county. Considering most of this county was desolate wildness, I didn't think that was the selling point they meant it to be. But I didn't bother finding out and chose the roasted chicken. Colleen ordered the same.

Our conversation was chilly if you'll pardon the pun. Or not. I just wanted it to end, it wasn't that long ago when things felt strained between us for the first time because of the tall dark and handsome bouncer. As tempted as I was to ask about the ghosts she hadn't seen, this trip was supposed to be fun, a renewal. A get away, but this strange, strangeness permeated our usual banter. I don't know if she knew what I was thinking. That it was really odd that she had not noticed any ghosts, but I desperately wanted to get back to some sort of normalcy.

"So that bar is next door. What do you say we go check it out?"

Colleen's eyes lit up, "Really? That would be fun as hell. You feeling frisky?"

"You know, I am kind of," I tried to mimic her sultry look, but I'm pretty sure I failed.

I left some money on the table, including a healthy tip, and we walked out the door leaving our awkwardness behind. Maybe she just didn't want to see another ghost. Or maybe she did and just didn't want to say. I had always assumed her reluctance to speak about her life involved trauma of some sort. I didn't want her to have to relive some painful memories simply to satisfy my own morbid curiosity about the afterlife. When I looked at it that way, my need to know appeared to be really selfish. I really am a dick sometimes. Probably why I like cats.

The bar was as dark and dingy as I expected it to be. Wonderfully creepy and totally backwoods stereotypically charming. The heads of dead deer hung on the walls; their glass eyes stared at us as if their fate were somehow our fault. I heard that banjo twang again, except this time not just in my head. It was coming from the speaker overhead. We laughed simultaneously, partly out of the delicious corniness of it, and partly out of relief that we seemed to be back on track.

We saddled up to the bar, where a grizzled bartender asked what we wanted. He didn't bother asking if we were locals, as we were obviously not. He was cordial until we ordered club sodas with a twist. Then his demeanor became decidedly darker. I didn't want to explain to him that neither of us had ever drank, or at least Colleen hadn't since she was alive.

When an extra big tip didn't seem to help, I turned to Colleen and said, "So what do you think we try just a smidge?"

She looked almost confused, "Really? I have no idea what that would do…. I mean now that I'm dead," she said that last part way too loud, but I don't think anyone heard. "And I didn't think you would ever want to try it. Are you sure?"

"I mean why the hell not. Our bed is right next door, and well….," I tried to look at her from under my eyelashes, "you only live once." We both started laughing, drawing entirely too much attention that time.

"What do we order?"

"I have no clue. Whatever we order, we should drink it slow." I pulled out my phone to google good first-time drinks but discovered that internet service was not a thing in this bar. This bar had exactly no bars. "Well, fuck. How about we just add a little vodka to this soda?"

"Sounds perfect!"

I got the bartender's attention and ordered two vodka sodas, which seemed to improve his attitude, albeit only slightly. When he set them down, we picked them up, clinked glasses and took two tiny apprehensive sips. We grimaced at the same time, tasting fire. Fifteen minutes later we had only brought the level of the liquid down in the glass a millimeter or so but were starting to feel it. We were comparing the sensations and found that they were similar. We were so wrapped up in the experience that we didn't notice the guy approaching us.

"Hey ladies," he said. He had a face that vaguely resembled a celebrity that I couldn't quite put my finger on. The rest of him was well, intriguing in a backwoods sort of way. His thin T-shirt struggled to contain his biceps, and his jeans were a work of art all on their own. He had short light-colored hair and a soft-looking well-kept beard.

"Hey yourself," Colleen said, and it was sexy when she said it. When I said that to Dom, it was very much not.

"Hello," I said managing to make a single word sound awkward. My belly was warm and my head a bit fuzzy. This handsome country bumpkin was making my nether regions warm too. Although, it's possible that it was just vodka. I looked at Colleen and we shared the same filthy thought. So far, Colleen had only been a voyeur. This would turn out to be a very different experience.

"I'm Alex."

18

Alex was not a local. Which ended up being a really good thing. He was only visiting some family and was planning on leaving early in the morning to start a very long drive to his home state. He was more than happy to accompany us to our room. Colleen and I didn't have more than just that one drink which also turned out to be a really good thing. The small amount of alcohol made us each a little bit goofy. Well, a bit more goofy than normal anyway. We were having fun. Alcohol makes a convenient excuse for bad decisions, at least that's what I always thought. But there was simply no way I could have known just how bad a decision taking poor Alex back to our room would be. But at least Margaret had fucked off and didn't see him come in with us.

So, it started out totally fun and normal. Just a couple of chicks double teaming a guy from the bar that they would never see again. Maybe not totally normal for some people. Especially when you consider that one of those chicks is dead, but it felt normal to us.

Since Colleen and I had never been with a guy at the same time, at least not when she was solid and able to participate, the logistics took some time to figure out. But when we did, it was amazing. Alex laid on his back, and graciously offered his face as a seat for me. His beard was as soft as it looked. Like the downy fur on a baby deer. Colleen had him in her mouth. I was in heaven, for a minute. Until he grunted and stopped moving his tongue abruptly. I lifted up slightly, thinking I might be smothering the guy, but when I looked down, I saw that something had gone wrong. Like really, really super-duper wrong.

Colleen sat up and wiped her chin, "Oh fuck."

I un-straddled Alex's face and turned to look at him. He looked the same way that Honey had when she was mimicking Paul in the VIP. Alex stared toward the ceiling, looking at nothing. His mouth was wide open. He looked like he was riding a rollercoaster and had his picture taken at the first big drop, face forever frozen in time. For all intents and purposes, he looked like he was having fun. The time of his life really. Or death apparently.

"What the actual fuck?" I said to Colleen, who had her head down, avoiding looking at me.

"Fuck, fuck, fuck," she whispered. "I'm sorry."

"Sorry for what?" But there was something deep down that told me I probably knew what.

She looked at me with an expression I had never seen her have, sorrow, pity, I'm not sure exactly. "I didn't mean to. I swear. I just got carried away."

"Dude, how do you kill someone with a blow job Colleen? Was he on something?" I knew that couldn't be the case though. Two dead guys dying the same way, was too much of a coincidence. I started to think that my ghost was a psychopath, but I couldn't figure how she could have killed them.

"I guess I have to tell you something. Please don't hate me. I'm not bad. I just can't help this sometimes. Well, all the time. But I've been trying. I meant to stop just before, but then it happened and I…" I had never heard her ramble this way. I was on the verge of a major freak out, my stomach roiled.

"Just tell me. What the fuck did you do?"

"I killed him."

"No shit Sherlock," I was scared and pissed.

"I'm not a ghost. Really. I think I'm something called a succubus."

"You mean like a sex demon? You fuck people to death?"

"Well, yeah, kind of. But not on purpose. And not people I love." She was looking down toward her immaculate breasts. She sounded tearful, but I didn't see any fall. "I didn't ever want you to know, Lacey. I love you. I have since you were a little kid. Please don't hate me."

"Hate you? What the fuck are you even? You've been lying to me," I was trying not to yell. "And now I'm probably going to prison. Were you ever even a person?" I don't even know why I asked that. I knew she wasn't. In fact, I probably had an inkling from the very beginning. No human looks like Colleen. She's a work of art, built like a goddess. Or a sex demon, I guess.

"I didn't lie. Not really. I…I just didn't want to lose you," she looked at me then and I began to cry. I was mad, and scared. Alex was silent. I looked at him and realized that I or we had some decisions to make. I was very grateful that we hadn't had any more than that one drink. My head was swimming, and I was going to puke. Again.

I ran to the bathroom and made it to the toilet this time. The vodka burned my throat again, as it had going down. My first drink in my whole life. In that moment I hoped it would be my last. Colleen came in and put her hand on the back of my neck. I was hurt and confused and pissed off, but her cool hand stopped my nausea.

I didn't want to go to jail, but I couldn't think of anything to do but call the police. There was no point in calling an ambulance. I closed my eyes and tried to stop the hurricane of my thoughts. I was totally fucked.

"It's going to be okay," Colleen said as she handed me a flowered hand towel. I wiped my mouth and face with it.

"How the fuck is it going to be ok Colleen?" I said through a veil of snot and tears.

"We don't have to call the police. The bar was empty, no one saw him come up to our room. He was leaving in the morning anyway."

"We can't just leave him here."

"No, we can't. But this place is surrounded by forest. Besides, don't you remember? He said he loved nature."

"Dump him in the woods? Surely you can't be serious. How would we even get him out there?"

"I am serious. And don't call me Shirley," she tried on a wry smile, but my frown told her I didn't appreciate the joke and her smile ran away from her perfect face. "There's plenty of time left before the sun comes up. And there's a laundry chute down the hall that goes to the basement. We can take him through there, and out to the woods."

"Do you think he'll fit through there?" I couldn't believe I was even thinking about going along with this. But he was already dead. I couldn't help him. I didn't want to go to jail for something I didn't do. And as is her habit, Colleen was making sense. A fucking demon. Literally.

"Not as he is."

I still sat on the bathroom floor. Afraid to stand up.

"Dude, I can't deal with this," I puked again.

"Don't worry. I got this. It's my fault. But I've been trying to figure out a way to not have them die, I swear. It just hasn't worked. They've all been accidents."

I believed her. I'm not sure what choice I had really. I could let her handle it or call the police and be locked up for the rest of my life. Although, if I told them a demon did it, I would probably spend my days doped up in a mental ward. I pulled the long chain that flushed the old timey toilet and laid on the floor with the towel over my face. If I laid here long enough, maybe I would just wake up and it would all just be a dream. Like a shitty ending to some novel. Colleen had gone into the main room, and I could hear her moving the body around. I kept my eyes closed and tried to stop thinking. I heard a heavy thud coming from the bathtub only a few feet from me, then the sound of the shower curtain sliding on its rod.

"There, he'll just chill in the tub for a few. Let me help you to the bed…. The other bed. Just keep your eyes closed. I'll make this all ok. I promise." She helped me up, carefully keeping the towel over my head. She guided me to the unsoiled bed and helped me get under the covers. She lifted the towel and kissed my forehead. "I will handle this. Whatever happens, you'll be ok. I love you." An icy tear landed on my cheek, and she replaced the towel. My world went dark, as by some miracle I fell asleep. When I woke up, the sun was shining. And both my demon and short-lived lover were gone.

19

Colleen

I learned from the world wide web that not only are birds not real, but that Succubae can put people to sleep. A very fortunate talent to have with a freaked out human lover and a dead one-night stand. I put Lacey to sleep with a kiss and dealt with Alex the only way I could think of. She wasn't just freaked out, but in danger of spending the rest of her life in prison. Of course, I would be with her, but that's not the point.

You already know that I didn't mean to do it. I know it's getting old, but seriously I don't know what the hell is wrong with me. One second, I'm just getting it on, and the next second, they're dead. I felt bad about Alex, he seemed like a good dude, but I felt worse about Lacey. But at least I handled the mess I made. It was a pretty big mess.

After she was asleep, I went invisible. I probably didn't have to. The place was totally dead, and there was still no sign of Margaret the Innkeeper. But I wanted to be as safe as I could. And if anyone did happen to see a free-floating tree limb saw and plastic garbage bags floating their way up to the only occupied room that night, it would just be another ghost story to tell. So, there's that.

Piece by piece, I dropped our unfortunate lover down the laundry chute. The maid must have done all the laundry and the sound each bag made as it hit the bare floor…. was unpleasant. Kind of a wet plop. Except for the head, that was more like a thunk followed by a bounce and roll. But at least it wasn't loud. Anyone listening would have thought it was an animal or something. Certainly not a sex demon disposing of a dismembered body. Getting those pieces out of the basement and into the forest was much trickier.

Locks are not usually an issue for me. Neither are doors and walls for that matter. But Alex was solid, so I had to toss him out the window, and then pick him up on the other side. The sun had started to come up and the roosters were crowing. There were people awake and doing outside chores. Although completely unintentional, I've grown somewhat accustomed to dead people. Hiding their bodies was a whole other can of worms. Worms would probably come into play at some point though. Getting all the bags, I think there were five or six, out in the forest without them being seen wasn't going to happen. There was plenty of forest around, but no way to access it without someone seeing a full trash bag cruising through the cool morning air on its own. You know, I would have probably done that town a favor if I had let my antics be seen. The ghost hunters and their TV producers would be there the next day. The amount of tourists would be insane.

There were several dumpsters behind some of the buildings. So, I carefully deposited a bag in each one. I didn't have to worry about fingerprints. And most of the garbage was food stuff and yard waste. So Alex ended up being close to nature anyway. See? It wasn't all bad. Each black plastic bag just looked like another bag of garbage, and the heavy lids should keep the animals out until they were dumped. And if not, well I think I remember him saying he liked animals too. It's probably what he would have wanted, if not really in a better place.

I washed out the tub, and replaced the saw, clean as a whistle back in the basement. There wasn't anything to tie Lacey to the body parts in the various dumpsters. Even if someone saw us take him back to the room, there was no evidence that he accidentally died in our room. At least that I can think of. But I've done plenty of research on the internet about such things. Forensics doesn't seem that complicated. After all the videos I've watched and stuff I've read, I'm surely an expert by now. There is so much information out there if you only know where to look.

Hiding stuff from the cops is not all that hard. I doubt that Taylor was Angel's first victim. That chick has probably taken out a ton of girls over the years, and the cops obviously haven't connected her to them yet. You'd think that they would at some point, have connected her to that nutty podcast. Not to mention she just acts like a psychopath. Sure, she's nice to the people that kiss her butt. Mostly. If anyone acts like someone who could easily kill people, on purpose, it's her.

20

When I woke up, the room was spotless, and Alex was gone. Colleen was too. Or at least I couldn't see her. I don't think I'm any kind of psychic, but I knew she was there. This place was old and drafty, but there is no mistaking that chill of hers.

"I know you're here." I didn't really. Not for sure. I had thought that she couldn't be invisible to me.

"I didn't think you would want to see me," a sad but somehow still sexy disembodied voice said.

"Well, you're terrible at hiding." I wished Bert and Ernie were as good at hiding as she was. The blue glittery dildo rested on the pillow next to me. We had taken them out to show Alex how they worked. He was impressed with our coordination.

Colleen materialized exactly where I thought she would. She was naked, because…well I don't know why. Probably the sex demon thing. As I looked at her, I felt kind of dumb thinking she was just a ghost. She looked human…ish. But there was a kind of surreal aspect to her. She was almost too perfect. Even supermodels have some flaw, or blemish. Something that makes them unique in some way. A slight imperfection that perfects their beauty.

Something that makes them human. Colleen didn't have that. She was the very embodiment of physical perfection.

It wasn't that I found out that she was a succubus, it was more that I acknowledged it. One of those little pieces of knowledge that hides in the back of your mind and pops up now and then for a split second. Not long enough to form a coherent thought. Then melts back into the recesses of your brain. Even if she had looked completely human, the way she avoided talking about her *life* was a pretty big clue. You didn't have to be Nancy Drew to figure that out. Throw in her uncanny sex appeal and powers of persuasion, and I wasn't so much dumb, as willfully ignorant. I might not have pinned her for a succubus or sex demon or whatever. But all the signs were there that she wasn't the spirit of a person that had once walked the earth.

I wonder if I even had a choice whether to fall in love with her. And that should bug the fuck out of me, and yet it doesn't. I guess it begs the question of how much free will plays into who we fall in love with. Maybe it doesn't at all. Love is a tricky and sometimes fickle thing that doesn't seem to lend itself very well to rules and rational thought. At least that's what I tell myself now, after having fallen in love with a demon that can't seem to help herself from killing people.

The ultimate irony is that I thought that I would get answers to so many of my unanswered questions about the afterlife from Colleen, and yet all I have is more questions. Like: is there even an afterlife? And where the fuck did Mary really go if anywhere?

"I'm sorry, Lacey."

I expected her to keep talking, but that was all she said.

"Well, we have an hour until breakfast. And well…I need some answers."

"Lucy! You have some splaining to do!" Colleen beamed a smile at me, testing the waters. I tried not to laugh. Like I tried really hard. And then laughed anyway.

"For real though. No more bullshit. Tell me everything. I mean everything. Lying by omission is still lying."

She had a sheepish, apologetic expression. One that was undeniably cute, but that really should have made me angry, but only made me horny. I made a mental note to look up the various talents and abilities of Succubae. There would need to come a point where I would have to find a way to resist her charms. Sometimes at least. I had grown quite fond of her charms.

"Is it really though?"

"Yes. It is. Seriously, no more fucking around. Everything, from the beginning."

She turned her eyes to the flowered and rumpled bedding we were sitting on and began to hopefully really, tell me everything. Bert and Ernie listened quietly.

"I didn't come from the Ouija board. I don't know how I came to find you. I'm not even sure where I came from before that. But I've been with you for a long time. Since you were a kid. There was nothing, and then there was you. My first memory is seeing you in the school library. You were scared. Lonely. I loved you immediately. Not in a sexy way. That came much later. But I saw how the other kids treated you. I wanted to protect you. And I did."

"So how do you know you're a demon?"

"The internet?"

I rolled my eyes.

"I know. But what else could I do? I was as lost as you when I found you. Lonely and looking for answers. It turns out that the internet is full of answers. Like did you know that putting garlic in your vagina is good for you?"

"No dude. Unless you're trying to deter pussy eating vampires. That's not ok ever. The internet is full of answers, but that doesn't mean they're the right ones." I almost added that vampires weren't real, but then realized that I was talking to a supernatural, not ghost, but maybe cum demon. So, I didn't think I could entirely discount the existence of vampires.

"Suit yourself. Any who, when you picked up that Ouija board, it seemed like a good time to introduce myself. The research I was able to do online all pointed to my being a succubus. I occasionally visited people when they were sleeping and absorbed their orgasms. Mostly guys. I didn't know what made me want to do that, just that I had to. And at first, I didn't realize that my visits weren't…ah…good for them."

"Ya think?" I pictured poor Alex. Although, I have to admit, he looked relatively happy to go that way.

"That's why I didn't do that to you. Until we met for real, after you were an adult. And I learned that a succubus *can* love, and don't kill those they do. Even after a bunch of wild sex. You're welcome."

I frowned at that, and she smiled, "Gee thanks." But really, it was nice to know that she did love me. Or I'd be dead. "Do I want to know how many people you've visited?"

"Probably not," she cringed. "But I think I would have died if I hadn't done that. It was really for your own good. I'm here to help you."

"I'm really not sure I want to know, but have you only killed people that you've visited?" She cringed again. "Tell me the truth." I wasn't fucking around. I didn't know if I was even capable of sending her away, but I certainly wasn't going to hang out willingly with a murderer. At least not a deliberate one.

"So, I may have helped one or two along, but not killed them directly. Just a little nudge."

"Oh fuck! What about Mary?"

"Ok, so in my defense, I was sure she was a bad person. And when she started to wake up when we were in her house, I helped her get back to sleep. Then I got into her dreams. I thought I could just keep her asleep, but then the dream got just a tad out of hand and took a bit of a sexy turn. Honestly, I didn't think the old lady had that in her. And then she just wasn't breathing anymore."

"So that's why we burned the house down."

"I mean we robbed her too. But really, I thought she was Nazi."

"Wait, what do you mean you thought?" There was that cringe again, but it came with a shrug this time. "Tell me."

"I saw in that cop's notebook that she was just a history buff. A collector of World War II stuff."

"So, we robbed an innocent old lady, and you orgasmed her to death, and then we burnt her house down?"

"On accident."

"What the actual fuck?" What do I even do with this information? I didn't have any doubt that she was telling me the truth though. She oozed remorse. And she had never been mean to anyone that I know of. Not even Richard.

I couldn't help but think that my poor social skills had gotten me into this mess. If only I peopled better. I might have found a real live life partner. "What else did you see in that cop's notebook Colleen?" This was definitively a question I didn't want to know the answer to, but it seemed important.

"Uh, he knows about Scott."

"What about Scott? Is he dead?"

"Yeah."

"Fuck me, Colleen."

"Ok!" She moved closer to me on the bed, but I stopped her. I'm actually kind of proud of that. It was the first time I had resisted. That alone gave me hope that I had at least some control of my own.

"No dude. Fuck me, as in I'm fucked."

"Ok, he isn't dead."

"The truth."

"He is. I wasn't satisfied after you left him, and I went back later that night. But I swear, I tried not to kill him. I get kind of carried away, and then before you know it." She threw her head back in a frozen scream, and still managed to look sexy.

"So, the cop suspects me of killing Mary and Scott?"

"That's what it looks like," she looked sorry again. But brightened and said, "I could pay Detective Shelton a nighttime visit?"

"That would be murder for sure," although, I thought I might warm up to the idea if things started to look really bad. Or worse, I guess. Things were definitely already bad. "Colleen, I need you to not kill anyone. At least for a little while. Probably forever."

"I might die though."

"You can't keep killing people. We'll figure this out somehow." Or not, but an idea hit me. "Hey, what about a sperm bank?"

She looked thoughtful, "Mmmm, I wonder. I'll have to do more research." I frowned at her. I was starting to have doubts about her research.

"Let's just table that for now. I guess I don't have to ask about Paul. What about Taylor?" It was my turn to cringe.

"Nope. I think that was all Angel and her illumiTwati. See, I'm not the asshole here."

"You're kind of the asshole. An inadvertent demonic asshole maybe, but still the asshole." I almost asked what she did with Alex and decided that not only did I not want to know, but it would be much safer if I didn't. That way if the police asked if I knew I could honestly say I didn't. "You still think she killed her?"

"I do. And she did it on purpose. That definitely makes her the asshole. Maybe we could pin all the murders on her?"

"That certainly sounds like a good idea. But I don't know how we would make that happen. Right now, I'm really worried about the police. Not to mention you killing anyone else."

She looked down again, "I'm here to take care of you. To love and protect you." Her tone took an unfamiliar serious tone, "I won't let you go to jail. If it comes to that, I'll go solid and take the heat."

I didn't know what to say to that. She was the one responsible for all this, but the thought of her spending even one moment in jail made my heart break. But it would probably be only a moment. I didn't think bars or walls would be much of an issue for her. I wondered if they could even book her. She never existed. No birth certificate, fingerprints. My head was spinning, and I was hungry.

"Let's go down and get our breakfast and get home. Richard is going to be pissed."

"Dick."

I rolled my eyes at my succubus.

21

Breakfast was delicious, but as hungry as I was, I found it hard to eat. Colleen didn't make it any easier either. She picked up a pancake, held it up to her mouth and poked a hole in it with her tongue. Then flicked it in and out suggestively. Margaret, being the only other living soul in the house, watched as I tried not to laugh. I don't think she thought it was as funny as I did.

I wondered if we should just run away. Just pick up and bail. Getting another job as a stripper wouldn't be hard. I almost proposed just that, but if the police were really suspicious, up and moving would only make it worse. I think I'm pretty smart, but I wasn't entirely sure that I was smart enough to hide from the cops. If I skipped town, would they call in the FBI? It's not like I had any real ties to my home though. No real friends. Just the house. Unless I wanted to abandon it, waiting around to sell it would kind of defeat the purpose of running and hiding. I didn't have much of a choice but to face whatever was coming next. Continuing with the relentless irony that is my life, the one thing that kept me from a full-blown panic attack and breakdown, is what caused all the crap in the first place.

Colleen, my cum demon. Her intentions were good. I think. And if anything, at least I wasn't alone.

And then there was Angel. Taylor was missing. And after listening to several podcasts along with what Colleen had said she had found and heard, it wasn't hard to believe she had killed someone. Angel was a thundercunt of epic proportions. I didn't have to search the internet to know that often strip clubs were fronts for all sorts of shady stuff. Any kind of business that ran on cash like that was an easy way to launder money. I mean HBO had a whole show on how the mafia cleaned their money through a strip club. It was fictional, but the best fiction all contains some truth. Angel had a whole staff of big guys at her disposal. Getting rid of a stripper wasn't much of a stretch. All the girls were afraid of her, and the staff kissed her ass for a reason. I wasn't sure if the girls knew about the podcast cult thing, but I didn't think it really mattered whether they did or not. Either way I knew that Angel had something to do with Taylor not being around anymore. I didn't think there was much if anything we could do about it. But I thought that if anyone would be able to find a tangible link or evidence, it was Colleen.

I think Margaret was relieved when we finished breakfast. We grabbed our stuff from upstairs and took one last look around to see if we had left anything behind. Like blood, semen or a phone charger. Colleen had been very thorough. Cleaning up bodily fluids was apparently her thing.

Margaret didn't ask how our stay was. She wore a stony look on her face the entire time she was checking us out. She didn't even make eye contact. I think she thought we were lovers or something. As if. Her salty demeanor eased up however, when I paid the bill in cash. I thought about leaving a big tip too, but I didn't want to give her any more reasons to remember us.

The sky had gotten a little overcast by the time Colleen and I tossed our overnight bags in the car. She didn't really need a bag, but I had given her one along with some of my clothing so she would look more like a live person. I wasn't sure if I wanted to have her go solid anymore after that trip though. Her charms were hard enough to resist when she was see-through, and she wasn't an easy sight to forget. She sat in the passenger seat wearing a T-shirt and jeans of mine that didn't fit all that well. But she would go invisible again before we got home anyway. I drove much slower home than I had driving there. I didn't turn the radio on.

"Are you still mad at me?" Colleen asked. I should have been but wasn't. We had come this far. I just couldn't believe that she was a malignant being. A weird thing to say about a demon, but still true. I don't think she did any of that on purpose.

"Not really, I guess. But I need you to make me a promise that you will not visit anyone or try and gather any cum or dreams. None of that until we figure some stuff out."

"Ok. But what do I do if I have a craving?"

"Fight it. But for fuck's sake let me know if you can't. And we'll find you some or something. Hell, I don't know. We… I can't afford to have any more dead people around me. But maybe that detective won't be back. Mary was burnt to a crisp, and Scott died suddenly in his bed. I don't think he would have any real evidence tying me to either. Other than I had known them. Same thing with Paul. And that cop didn't seem to think there was anything suspicious. They won't find any marks or poison. Just sad coincidences."

"Accidents," she said.

"Well, they won't know that either. So maybe we don't have anything to worry about."

"What about Taylor? Angel killed her, I'm sure of it."

"What proof do we have? That she runs a podcast? That she is a real bitch to the girls and nice to the staff? I think she had something to do with Taylor being gone, but the last thing I want to do is talk to another cop. I'm really shitty at it anyway."

"You really are though." And she wasn't wrong.

"Even more reason for you to chill and not kill anyone." I took my eyes off the windy road for a second to look at her sternly, "Even accidentally." She smiled at me.

"But if you were able to find some sort of evidence tying her to Taylor, we could drop an anonymous tip." I didn't think for one second that turning Angel in would somehow make up for Colleen's inadvertent victims, but at least we would be doing the right thing for once. I was determined to figure out a way to live with my succubus without her killing people. Either that, or she might have to die, or whatever happens to Succubae when they don't feed. I couldn't stand that thought, it brought tears to my eyes and put a knot in my stomach. I turned on the radio and found something hard and loud we could both yell along with, and that thought kindly fucked off.

We got home and Richard was waiting by the door. Pissed, but not as much as I expected. He seemed happy to see me. He wound himself between my legs and I bent to pick him up. He nuzzled under my chin and licked my face. When I put him down, he simply turned his tail to Colleen without hissing. So, more progress. I went into the kitchen and saw that he still had a few nuggets of food left. I gave him a can of wet food and he was completely content again. Until Colleen made to pet him, he hissed at her, and went back to his food. They still had a long way to go to be friends, but maybe they would get there eventually.

I unpacked our stuff, and we hopped in the shower together. The drama from the night before, wasn't forgotten. But there wasn't anything I could do about any of it. I had a succubus girlfriend who had left a bunch of dead people in her wake. There was a killer at the club I worked at, but there wasn't much I could do about that at that moment either. I didn't feel great about the people who had died, but once again, what could I do about it? Nothing.

We emerged from our shower refreshed, and sort of renewed. It was afternoon, and I was hungry after not being able to eat much breakfast. I tossed on a pair of sweatpants and a T-shirt. Not the one from Scott though. I threw that one in the trash. Poor guy. Colleen had mentioned that she thought he might have had roofies in his pocket and was a real bad dude. But she had also thought that Mary was a Nazi, so I took that piece of information with a grain of salt. I ordered take out Chinese, my favorite, and we put on a terrible but mind-numbing horror flick.

Things felt normal again. Clearing the air with her was what we needed to do. Granted it wasn't all great. But what relationship doesn't have its issues? Ours was just a little more unique. At least compared to mainstream relationships. Probably par for the course in any human demon homosexual relationship. Sure, we still needed to figure out how to get her semen, without killing anyone. But semen isn't all that scarce if you know where to look. Guys were just giving it away.

I packed my pipe, and we passed it back and forth, giggling at the ketchup covered B-list actors on the TV screen. The movie was about a serial killer that had died, but his ghost came back to murder the people who had gotten him caught. It was hilarious. Richard snuggled up next to me on the couch. I was stoned as hell, and everything felt right with the world. Except for the dead guys. That still sucked, but I took one more hit and pretty much forgot about it.

A knock at the door pulled me out of my bliss. But only slightly.

"Ugh, I need to get a 'no soliciting' sign," I said to my very high demon girlfriend.

"You really do though. Don't get up, they'll go away." I hunkered down on the couch. Thinking maybe if I sunk low enough, they would give up and go away. Not that the person at the door would know that I was hiding in my couch. But logic at that moment was hard to come by.

The knock came again. Louder. It was almost six in the evening, a pretty damn rude time to be knocking on the door.

"I think I have to tell them to fuck off."

"What if it's girl scout cookies?"

Colleen shrugged her shoulders and went into ghost mode. I got up. Slowly. The knock came again as I got close to the door.

"Hang on, I'm coming. You'd better have cookies," I said as I unlocked the door and pulled it open.

Detective Shelton stood outside. He wasn't wearing his sunglasses this time.

"Sorry, no cookies. But I have some more questions."

"Fuck," I meant to say in my head, but it came out of my mouth instead.

22

My living room was thick with pot smoke, like I had been having a smoke off with Snoop Dogg. One of those horrible moments when I wished I wasn't so high. This guy had the worst timing ever. Colleen was right behind me. I was hoping she would have an idea. I was lost. But I heard her start to snicker, and immediately changed my mind and hoped she wouldn't have an idea. But it was too late. She did.

I started to say something other than 'fuck' in greeting, but Shelton's eyes got heavy. Like he had just taken a hit off the pipe. Then he started to slump. Colleen went solid and caught him before he fell to the ground. She moved to put him in one of the chairs on the porch. I didn't know she was so strong. My knees felt like they were melting.

"What the hell are you doing?"

"I put him to sleep!" She beamed, "I didn't even know I could do it like that. I thought they had to be in bed or already half asleep."

"Dude, how long will he be out? We can't leave him on the porch. Oh my god, he looks dead." My heart was pounding. The homicide detective's unmarked sedan was parked in front of my house. I looked around to see if there was another car or cop around. There wasn't one, at least not that I could see. If there were they would see two very stoned chicks, one in sweatpants, and the other naked, as naked as a sex demon.

"I think as long as I want," she said.

"Will he die?"

"Not if I stay out of his dreams and his pants."

"Fuck. Let's bring him in and put him on the couch." That seemed better than leaving him outside. At least until we could figure out what to do with him. I looked around again to see if any of my neighbors might see us carry an unconscious cop looking guy into the house. The construction crew that was tearing down Mary's house had gone home for the day. The street was deserted. But that knowledge didn't do much for my squishy knees and hammering heart.

Colleen hooked her arms under his shoulders to support his top half. His head lolled to the side and his tongue rolled out. He looked dead, I really hoped Colleen wasn't wrong about killing him. I picked up his feet, and we carried him inside and set him carefully down on the couch. I heard him moan softly as Colleen tucked a pillow under his head. My heart jumped off the ledge and into my stomach, but he didn't seem to wake up. I closed and locked the front door.

"Dude." That's all I could say. I was pacing the living room. Colleen was busy opening all the windows, she left the blinds drawn so no one could see in, mitigating the ventilation. "Duuuuuuude." I said again, in lieu of plan, then added, "fuck," for good measure.

"It's going to be okay. I promise. Trust me." Trust was as elusive as rational thought was at that moment. She left the room, and I heard the door in the kitchen that led to the tiny garage open and close. I had no idea what she might have been going in there for, there wasn't much there except for an exercise bike I didn't use along with some old Christmas decorations. And Christmas was still months away. When she returned with a floor fan, I felt slightly stupid. But some semblance of thought returned to me, and I picked up a stick of incense, put it in a holder that was decorated with pot leaves, and lit it. First step in operation *what the hell do we do* was complete. I had no clue about the second.

"I know what you're thinking, and he's not dead. Just really asleep." She was wrong that time, I wasn't thinking anything. In fact, I was proud of myself that I had thought to get the incense. There was nothing after that. Unless you count the endless stream of *dude, fuck, dude, fuck, dude*. "When it clears out in here, we'll wake him up and tell him that he fainted," she smiled.

"Great. Then what?" I wasn't even being sarcastic, I really wanted to know.

"We'll answer his questions. Just like last time," she said. "No biggie."

"No biggie my ass."

"Your ass is beautiful, but if you don't want it to get bigger you can always dust off the bike in the garage." She smiled as I scrunched my eyebrows together.

"That's not what I meant. I'm going to screw this all up even worse."

"You won't. They're already cleaning up Mary's house. You were long gone before Scott had his accident. There's nothing to worry about. Just stay calm."

"I'd have to be calm, to stay calm. And I'm a long way from calm."

"I could get in his dream?"

"So… that would be murder…."

"Maybe technically, I guess."

"Yes, that would be technically murder."

"Ok fine. But we'll need to wake him soon."

She was right, I couldn't leave him there forever. I sent Colleen into the kitchen for a glass of water and a cold wet cloth. When She got back, I placed the folded cloth on his forehead. He looked so peaceful. I almost didn't want to wake him. No, that's not true. I definitely didn't want to wake him. But I had to. I took a few deep breaths and gave a nod to Colleen who dematerialized. When I could see the wall through her, she came over to the sleeping cop and put a hand on his chest. Then she retreated to the corner of the room where she gave me an enthusiastic double thumbs up. Detective Shelton opened his eyes.

"Hey there," I said softly. I pressed the cloth into his forehead. I'm not sure if that's what you should really do if someone faints, but I hoped it would give the impression that he fainted and wasn't put to sleep by a succubus. "You fainted when I opened the door."

"Uh…I did?" He sounded groggy, but not as groggy as I would have liked. I didn't want him at his sharpest. He sat up and looked around. The thin trail of smoke rose up from the incense, and I thought that the weed smoke was pretty much gone by then. I couldn't smell it anymore. "Did you have a smoke out with Snoop in here?" Ok, so maybe I was still too stoned to smell it.

"Yeah, you caught me relaxing," I let out a laugh that I hoped sounded embarrassed and not guilty. "Are you ok? How do you feel?"

"Fine, I think. Weird. I feel like I just woke up from a nap. Lucky, I didn't hit my head. You must be pretty strong to have carried me inside all by yourself." I felt like I was going to puke.

"I work out." I lied. Colleen gave me another two thumbs up from her corner. I think it would have been helpful if she hadn't been naked though. It was awfully distracting. I handed him the glass of water and he took a sip. He blinked a couple of times, then removed his notebook and pen from his jacket pocket.

"Well thank you. Let's get to it. I really only have a couple more questions."

"Ok."

"You got this!" Colleen said. I didn't think I had it at all.

"Do you remember a few months back meeting a guy named Scott at the Underground Bar and Grill?" he asked, with no hint of sleepiness.

"I think so."

"You were wearing his shirt when I was here last."

"Oh yeah. I remember him. Vaguely."

"The bartender said you went home with him, but you only remember him vaguely?"

"He wasn't that memorable if you catch my drift." Colleen shook her head violently back and forth. "I mean…he was just a quickie," I said, not making it any better. But I guessed that slut was better than murderer.

"Do you know what time you left his house that night?"

"Um…around midnight…ish" I didn't know, I looked to Colleen who shrugged her shoulders. She creeped up behind him to peer into his notebook.

"Are you aware that Scott passed away that night?" Colleen abruptly moved from behind him to behind me and blew a cold breath on my neck, causing me to inhale sharply. As if I was shocked. Sometimes she really does help.

"Oh no! What happened?"

"That's what we are trying to find out. He was fine when you left?" Colleen moved back to the notebook to see what he was writing. She looked up and gave me another two thumbs up, while her naked breasts framed his head. He shivered. She went back to the corner.

"He was. I ubered home and didn't hear from him again. Guys. Am I right?" I rolled my eyes. His head tilted to the side a little as he looked up from his notebook to me. I just smiled back.

"You recently began working at the Embers Gentleman's Club, is that correct?"

"Uh, yeah. Just til I get through college."

He frowned, "You're not enrolled in college right now." I guess he must have checked.

"I'm saving up," I smiled with too many teeth.

"And you were there when a customer passed away in the VIP room?" I wondered how the hell he would know that, probably the detective thing. But not a development I was excited about.

My smile dissipated, "I was. But I didn't kill him." His eyes widened and Colleen cringed. My palms became slick, and my voice trembled. I thought we might have to kill him after all. "I mean the cop said that he just died. He was fine when I left him though." I felt the cashew chicken I had just eaten start to dance a jig in my stomach. I'm sure innocent people barf all the time when they're talking to cops.

"What made you think I thought he was killed?" He sounded genuinely curious.

"Uh…nothing, I guess." I thought I was fucked for sure.

"You do seem to have a lot of deaths around you in a very short amount of time."

My brain finally gave up the ghost and went rogue, "Angel the cunty door girl killed Taylor." Colleen cringed again, but then in a flash, she was back behind him, and he fell asleep.

23

"Oh god, do we have to kill him now?"

"Not unless you really want me too, but I think we can still pull this off."

"Can't you do something about his memory? Like that alien movie where they use that memory erasing gadget? Maybe, just get rid of that last sentence?"

"No. It doesn't work like that. I'm a succubus not Will Smith. The only way I could get rid of his memory would be to… well, you know."

"I don't think we're there…" I said, but wanted to leave my options open, "yet."

"We could just tell him about Taylor and Angel and the podcast. Maybe even plant a seed of suspicion toward Paul?"

"That doesn't sound half bad. Kind of a two fer. Distract him from me and put him on Angel, at the same time? What did you see in his notebook?"

"That he is just covering his bases. He has a note that Scott, Paul and Mary all died of natural causes. He does a great doodle of a dog too."

"He would probably be a shitty cop if he didn't ask some questions, given that I was probably the last person to see all of those dead people. I wonder if he will be suspicious that he keeps fainting though?" I asked.

"So what? Why would he think you made him faint? If anything, I think it will help. Trust me, this is all going to work out just fine. Mentioning Taylor was probably not a great move though." There was that trust word again.

"I'm thinking I'm going to fuck this up."

"You'll do fine. Talk slow. If your mouth doesn't run away with you, this will all be over, and we'll celebrate with Bert and Ernie when it's all over." She gave me that devious smile from under her eyelashes that went straight to my crotch. Only Colleen could make me horny while I was trying to not to have a panic attack and not throw up. "And if not, I'll come see him in his dreams." She smiled again, and her warmth, the only kind she seemed capable of spreading hit me again. It was a completely inappropriate feeling but not totally unwelcome. Being inappropriately horny was the only thing keeping me from totally losing it.

For just a minute I wondered if I should let her go solid, I say *let her* as if I had any control over her at all, I had no illusions that I did. Colleen was her own demon for sure. But she did stay calm when things got scary. Maybe because she was the one always causing the scary stuff. I was sure she could handle all this better than I could. Being able to disappear whenever she wanted was probably a big factor. That and the fact that she didn't take a whole lot of stuff seriously. Ultimately, I thought that Colleen showing up, with no history, no record, no fingerprints or anything else to legitimize her would only serve to make the detective more suspicious. Besides, according to his notebook, he wasn't all that suspicious anyway. It was best to keep it from getting more complicated than it already was.

Colleen woke him up again, and I realized that I only thought I was ready, but then I wasn't. My legs were shaking, and my knees were still full of jelly. I figured as long as I didn't stand up, I might be ok. I was sitting on one side of the sofa, while the detective was slumped backward on the other. He moaned a little as he opened his eyes and sat up.

"You fell out again. Maybe you should have that checked out? Could be that sleeping disease." I thought that sounded very calm and reasonable. So far so good. He blinked at me curiously.

"I'm sorry. I don't know why that keeps happening. I should call someone to drive me."

"No!" I yelled, not sounding suspicious at all. In my defense, the last thing I wanted was more cops. He looked at me weirdly. "I mean, I'm sure you're fine. Here… have some more water," I handed him the glass again. He looked at it as if it were full of turpentine and set the glass on my coffee table. He looked at his notebook which had fallen in his lap when Colleen put him to sleep for the second time, as if he had forgotten all about it. He picked it up, looked at it and picked up where he left off. Where I left off. Until then, I still had hope that he might not have remembered what I said before he fell out again, but those hopes were dashed when he opened his mouth.

"What were you saying about the door girl?" If I had only kept my mouth shut, he would have closed his notebook and fucked off. He didn't suspect me in any of the *natural* deaths, but of course, I had to complicate things by bringing up Angel. On the plus side, it might get her caught.

"Ok, so I wasn't sure how to say this," that was true. "But last week, this new dancer named Taylor, probably not her real name, was crying about something Angel had said or did to her. And the girls were all freaked out, and then she was just gone." I was talking too fast, but completely helpless to stop. "I heard someone say that she had been taken out."

"Taken out as in murdered? Like the mob?"

"Well, yeah. But then I found this podcast, called Dark Angel. The door girl's name is Angel by the way, and she was talking about taking out her enemies that are trying to stop the apocalypse." He was staring at me, and I hoped he couldn't feel me shaking through the sofa.

"And you think that this door girl, Angel, is behind the podcast and a dancer's disappearance?"

"Yup. And… She wasn't very upset when they found the dead guy. I don't know but I wondered if she could have poisoned him or something?"

"And why would she do that?" Honestly, I had no clue. I knew I wasn't making sense. When Colleen and I were talking about it, it all seemed so obvious. It all seemed reasonable. Now explaining to a cop, it sounded a bit tin foil hat-ish. But he seemed hooked on my every word, so at least the distraction was working.

"I don't know. But I think you should look into it. Taylor is missing and there is something really wrong with Angel." Probably not a great idea to tell the cop how to do his job. I thought about telling him that she did the books and that maybe the mob *was* involved or something. But that seemed way too much. If there was anything to that, he would find it. Not to mention if the owner *was* some sort of crime boss, I didn't want to be the one caught snitching. And I was assuming he was taking me seriously at all. Maybe he would just think I was nuts, which I didn't think was a terrible outcome either.

"What else did you hear on this podcast and how do you know it's her?" Great question. I think Detective Shelton was probably pretty good at his job. Damnit.

"Well… it sounds a lot like her. The girls are really afraid of her, and the staff kisses her butt. She is selling magical protection stuff too and talking about taking people out." I was rambling again and hoping I was making some sort of sense. I looked at Colleen in the corner who grinned and gave me another thumbs up. I was expecting the detective to ask more questions, but he closed his notebook and stowed it in his pocket.

"Well, I'll check it out. That's all I have for now." For now? I wanted to barf. "I'll get in touch if I find anything or have any more questions." He stood up.

"Ok." I started to stand, but my legs wouldn't cooperate, and I fell back on my ass to the sofa. I giggled like I was totally freaking out talking to a cop about a bunch of dead people. He offered a hand to help me up. I took it, and he helped me stand. Somehow, I made it to the door to show him out.

"It's probably a good idea if you stay in town in case I need to talk to you again." That actually sounded like a terrible idea. House be damned, I wanted to run away.

"Oh sure. I have to work anyway."

"Huh…" he said questioningly. "You're not afraid of the door girl?" He raised an eyebrow.

"Oh yeah, terrified. But I've really been killing it there," I said, and my eyes went wide as I realized what had just come out of my mouth. Seriously, I should just have my tongue removed.

"Ok, well… have a good rest of your evening."

I closed the door and ran to the bathroom to puke.

24

I never really thought of myself as a puker. But then again, I'd never been investigated by the cops for a string of deaths either. It was becoming pretty inconvenient. Not to mention gross. Colleen didn't seem to mind. She held my hair back with one hand, while the other was on the back of my neck.

"I thought I had it in the bag, until I opened my big dumb mouth," I said and dry heaved for what I hoped would be the last time. My high had worn off, adding to my misery. "What is wrong with me?"

"You're human," Colleen said. "So, what if he looks into Angel? We… you probably did a good thing. No more people will die for insulting her, and her grift will probably get shut down. Your big mouth is a hero!"

I sat back from the bowl. I'm not a clean freak, but I had to admit that barfing in my own toilet was preferable to the one at the strip club. Colleen got down on the floor with me and put her arms around me. A cold hug, that felt warm somehow.

"I feel like an idiot, not a hero. I'm supposed to work tomorrow. Maybe I shouldn't go in?"

"No, you should. That way you don't look like a snitch or murderer. Like you're normal."

"Dude none of this is normal. Pretty much as of three years ago," I said and immediately felt like a dick. Colleen lowered her head, wounded. "I'm sorry. I didn't mean that."

"It's true though. I've made things hard for you."

"No, you didn't. I mean, you did. But I love you. Who knows what I would be doing without you? I'd probably be working a 9 to 5 and being a bitch to everyone because I hate my life. But instead, I'm a stripper with a demon for a girlfriend. For real, what would be better?"

"You mean that?" She lit up.

"Of course, I do," I gave her a kiss on the lips, but she pulled back.

"How about you brush your teeth, and we go fool around a bit?" It would seem that demons aren't immune to bad breath. I did as I was asked, and just like that everything was good again. Of course, if I'm being honest with myself, it's more likely just a product of her influence than everything actually being good again. Colleen's a kind of a demon placebo, but I can't say that I cared all that much.

When I woke up late the next morning, well more like early afternoon, Colleen was lying next to me. I rolled over and snuggled up next to her cool form. The dream I had been having hadn't totally drifted away yet. As I closed my eyes, pieces of it struggled to stay in focus and melted into the half sleep state I was occupying. I was snuggled up to someone. Curiously, someone warm, and bigger, whose scent was like fall rain and sandalwood. They were behind me, spooning me with their arm around me, holding me close. Protecting me. A smile crept to my face.

Something heavy landed on top of me and jolted me all the way awake. Richard was hungry, and annoyed that he could see the bottom of the dish. Colleen rolled over and petted his head, which he allowed. Albeit begrudgingly. I got up and padded to the kitchen. Still thinking about my dream, which insisted on lingering. I started the coffee and filled Richard's dish. I stretched and yawned, and realized that the person I had been snuggling with in my dream was Dom. A strange sense of guilt washed over me. Totally unreasonable. I had nothing to feel guilty about. I barely knew the guy. He was insanely attractive, that was it.

I brought coffee to Colleen in bed this time. She took it with a smile that brought back that odd guilty feeling. I stuffed it. I didn't need anything to ruin this afternoon. After a good night's sleep, things felt calmer than they had. Not quite normal, but I don't think normal was ever going to be my jam. Things didn't seem as complicated. Colleen had opened the laptop and had a video playing. Something about aliens having built the pyramids. Why is it always aliens?

"What if I'm an alien?" Colleen said thoughtfully.

"Nah. You'd be green, I'm almost positive."

"Well, the most important thing about research is keeping an open mind."

"But not so open that your brains fall out. Carl Sagan said that."

"Probably because he was an alien." I rolled my eyes.

I finished my coffee and got out of bed to get ready for work. It didn't take long, as it was so dark in the club that even half-assed make-up looked good. I ate a light dinner and headed to work. Colleen in tow.

We walked in, and Angel for some reason wasn't as salty as usual. I was immediately suspicious. She was almost cordial. Well, not cordial, but she pretty much ignored me and skipped the passive aggressive compliments. So relatively cordial. It was unnerving, a calm before the twat storm I wondered. I nodded to Rick as

I walked to the dressing room. There were a few girls getting ready for the night shift. They had been chattering away, but a hush came over them as I walked in. I figured as the new girl it was chatter that I wasn't privy to yet. I can't say that I minded much though, I had plenty of drama in my life as it was. The last thing I needed was to get caught up in locker room gossip. I stripped and put on my bikini and lip gloss. I was about to check in, when the whispers I had been trying to ignore wriggled their way into my ear.

"She was the last to dance…" was all I heard as the two girls stopped talking to give me simultaneous side eye glances. Great. I assumed that Lexus had started this sweet little rumor that I had somehow killed Paul. I wish they would make up their minds, either my lap dances were too shitty to give the guy a heart attack or were so good I killed him with his own raging boner. The strip club dressing room was bringing back memories of middle school. I didn't bless them with my acknowledgement of their shit talking and walked out to check in with Lars.

"Hey there kid. How ya doing?" he said, without looking at me. I didn't get the feeling that he cared at all about the shit talking.

"I'm pretty good, all things considered," I smiled at him, although he still wasn't looking at me. He picked up the mic and started to introduce the next girl. He pointed to his list to show me that I had a few more girls before I was up while speaking. I'll admit, I was impressed by his multitasking abilities. But maybe more so with his lack of need for small talk. He seemed to be as bad at people as I was. A misanthrope with antisocial tendencies. I liked him.

Colleen had left me at some point. She didn't say where she was going, but I figured she was looking for dirt on Angel. If Detective Shelton came back, it would be helpful to give him something other than a half-baked conspiracy theory. Assuming he hadn't just thought I was full of shit in the first place. I looked around at the decent amount of customers on the floor, when I noticed Dom at the entrance to the VIP room. It seemed like a good time to say something stupid to him, so I walked over and said "Hi".

"Hi yourself," he said making the kind of eye contact that made me want to faint. Better than barfing.

"How's it going tonight?" I said, not stupidly. Maybe I was learning?

"Not bad, bit of drama. But that's normal."

"Ha! Normal. I'm not normal at all." Smooth move… ex-lax, I thought and rolled my eyes at myself. If I was smart, I would have walked away then. But no. "What's the drama?" possibly the stupidest thing I could have said. I was trying to avoid the drama, not step in it.

"I guess you've been here long enough to know. One of the girls refused to pay Angel what she asked, and Angel is causing her problems now."

"What do you mean?" Now I was curious enough to step in the pile of strip club drama. This seemed like pertinent information.

"Angel tries to get money from the some of the new girls if she thinks they're vulnerable to keep them on the good shifts. The owner and staff let her get away with it, because she does the books, but also gives them a cut. Every once in a while, when a girl won't pay…well…it can get bad." I felt the drama squishing between my toes.

Any lingering doubt I had about Angel killing Taylor dissolved. She did it. I could only hope that Colleen was getting something we could take to Detective Shelton. I went about my night, smiling at Angel and the shit talkers. I could hardly wait to tell Colleen what Dom had said and find out if she had found anything. Although, on the plus side, Angel hadn't tried shaking me down for money.

As soon as we pulled out of the parking lot, I said, "Angel shakes down the new girls for money to get better shifts. And Dom said that it can get *really bad* if they refuse. Angel killed Taylor for sure."

24

Colleen

So, I'm trying not to be a liar, even by omission. Even if I'm not totally sold that lying by omission counts as a lie. But I think I came close to losing my Lacey. Even as a succubus, my influence can only go so far. I want her to genuinely love me. I know that I do, because otherwise she'd be dead. If only I could find a way to love everyone, then no one would die. But honestly, humans can be very hard to love sometimes. I found some stuff out, and I'm afraid that if I keep it from her, she'll be mad at me for not telling her, but if I tell her I'm almost sure she'll be mad at me.

I saw her talking to Dom, a guy I wish would go away. Yeah, I'm jealous, if you must know. But you should see the guy, he's a work of art in the flesh. Like a mocha version of Davinci's David. He's almost hard to look at, and I would much rather he stay away from my girl. Once this whole thing with Angel and the cops is over, I may have to do something about him. Maybe pay him a nocturnal visit. And yes, that would be murder. Technically. But it would be my only intentional one.

Except for Vivian. And done out of love, not malice. Maybe just a touch of malice. But at least he would enjoy it. Mostly.

I wasn't happy when I saw him talking to her. But not just because of my jealousy, but I question his intentions and truthfulness. Most of the staff completely bow down to Angel, either out of fear or respect. Dom does not. And I'm not sure why. There is something off about him. Something that I can't put my finger on. But I will find out.

But my dilemma now is about what I did find out. And whether I should tell Lacey or not. She's fine navigating the strip club without me. And she doesn't even need me to influence guys to make money. She's doing just fine on her own merits. So, I left her to do a little snooping. I lurked in the office and dressing room, and no one had any idea I was there. Funny thing about the club, they keep it ridiculously cold in there. No one notices a cold draft when I'm around.

It was in the office that I made the discovery that I don't want to tell her about. Mostly because it doesn't make me look all that great. Taylor wasn't taken out. She's very much alive. She's working the day shift. Angel put her there, and it sucks, but she's not dead. My bad. Again. But to some girls working day shift is a fate worse than death. Really. I didn't find this on the internet, but heard some girls and staff talk about it. Strip clubs have some strange customs and practices. Like the air blasting all the time in the dressing rooms and offices. That is done to encourage the underdressed entertainers to spend more time on the floor where they aren't freezing their asses off. Their asses being essential to their job. Another thing is the tips. Not much of a surprise, but money talks. In most businesses, you don't tip your boss or managers, but that's not how it works in the club. If you want to be treated well, it's cash or in some cases ass. And occasionally grass.

The hierarchy in the strip club can be boiled down to the shifts. Namely day and night shift. Night shift is where the money is, and so there is a line drawn there between the elites and the serfs. Lacey was new, young and attractive and so was automatically placed on the night shift. Taylor bitched about having to pay for the privilege. I know, the nerve. But also, rightfully, pointing out the unfairness of it all. And so, she was punished. Taken out or taken off, the night shift.

It's a messed-up business, but nothing I could really find out about on the internet. I had to be there, unnoticed, to do this research. In person, sort of. It's a really good thing that Lacey had me to look out for her. And another good reason to take out Dom, should he become problematic. Every stripper should have a helpful demon friend.

I also found out that Angel not only does the books but cooks them too. And I'm fairly sure that she's fucking the owner. I have no desire, however, to confirm that by actually watching that happen, so you'll just have to accept my supposition. So, I know that Angel isn't a killer but *is* a greedy Cuntface. I didn't get confirmation about the podcast, but it seems in line with her general Modis operandi. And there is still the business of the weird altar I found in the cabinet. If that doesn't scream culty podcaster I don't know what does.

So, do I tell her? Or no. I haven't read a lot about relationships, and the stuff I have read makes *me* want to barf. Soul mates and crap. Who even knows if we have souls? But the one piece of advice that seems consistent is honesty. I think if I want to keep her, I need to swallow my pride and tell her that I was wrong. Although even if she were to tell me to leave, I would just go invisible and haunt her again, because what else am I going to do?

25

Colleen didn't respond to the news that we had been right the whole time right away. That her research had actually paid off. And that we might catch a killer. We really would be heroes. She just kept looking at the road as I drove home.

"What's up?" I asked, but then I remembered I had been talking to Dom. "You aren't mad that I was talking to Dom, are you?"

"There's something off with that guy," she said still looking ahead.

"Yeah, that he's hella hot."

"No. Something else." She paused, and I was waiting for her to elaborate, but then she said, "I have to tell you something. I'm afraid you're going to be mad at me." I wasn't sure if I was ready for another confession. That last one had been a doozy.

"Well spit it out then."

She brightened and looked at me, "Spitting is rude. I always swallow."

"Dude, for real now. Just tell me. I won't promise I won't get mad, but I'll listen." I was thinking I was probably going to be mad. She darkened again. Not a great look for her by the way. Especially knowing that she is a demon. When Colleen got upset, there was this heaviness that came over her in a way that you couldn't forget what she was. I wasn't afraid of her when she got like that, but part of me wondered if I should be.

"Angel isn't a killer. Taylor isn't dead. She's working the day shift."

"Huh…." I paused. "So, I lied to a homicide detective who was investigating mysterious deaths that all seemed to have a connection to me?" Not a good look. And I was kind of mad.

"Yeah, but now he'll think you're just nuts. And it's not like she's an awesome person. She shakes down the girls for money to keep their place on night shift. And if they don't pay, it does get bad, just not dead bad. And she's cooking the books for the club. I don't know the specifics, but it looks like plain old tax evasion. I didn't hear anything about the owner being involved in crime, just a typical tax dodger. But she's definitely the leader of the illumiTwati!" That damned smile came back.

"Did you find out if that podcast was her?" I was hopeful, we could still be heroes taking down a grifter and possible death cult leader.

"I didn't, but I'm almost positive she is. You heard her on the podcast. So, you didn't totally lie to the detective. And he might find some dirt on her anyway. We did a good thing." Colleen and her good things, I needed to have a long talk with my demon about ethics.

"Ugh, well I hope he found her alive and just thinks I'm bonkers. This is such a mess."

"But are you mad at me?" That darkness again, and maybe it kept me from answering completely honestly.

"No. You made a mistake. But there isn't any evidence according to the cop's notebook, so I really shouldn't have anything to worry about. Right?" she lit up again.

"Nope! I think it's all good in the hood! There is no forensics, nothing and no evidence of foul play at all. Just a rash of sudden deaths that you happened to be kind of close to." I frowned at her, and she smiled.

We got home and Richard was waiting as usual. He let me pick him up and snuggle him before I let him down so I could fill his dish. Exhausted, I had a quick snack and crawled into bed with Colleen. She was waiting for me, naked, but all she wanted was to snuggle. An odd development. I happily fell asleep in her arms.

I dreamed again of Dom. This time it wasn't as pleasant. Or at least it didn't start out that way. I was being chased by someone or something I can't remember. He swooped in from above on black wings and plucked my pursuer up. I watched as he flew them up in the air and dropped them. They landed with a splat, destroying any chance I may have had of identifying them. Dom then took me in his arms and folded his wings around us. I awoke with a flaming ache between my legs that until then, only Colleen had been able to induce. When I turned to see her next to me, I felt that familiar and totally unwelcome sense of guilt.

"Good morning," she smiled, doing nothing for that ache.

"Good morning yourself," I smiled back. Trying my best to send the memory of that dream back to where it came from. I've never put a lot of weight into dreams. I've always considered them just brain garbage. Just a mind wandering with no point or meaning as the body rests and recovers from the bullshit of waking life. But there are always those dreams that challenge that line of thinking and linger long after waking up.

She kissed me, and her hand wandered down where that needy ache was coming from. I sighed and returned the favor. We tangled ourselves in the sheets, until we were both panting and spent. I loved our romps. Lived for them. Just pure raw physical pleasure that erased all my pains and troubles. Fingers, tongues and lips all moving toward one goal. But this felt different than our usual play. It felt like love making. I'm no kind of a romantic. Never have I dreamed of pina coladas or getting caught in the rain. I avoid romance novels of any kind, and the thought of watching a rom com makes me more nauseous than talking to the police about dead guys. And just to put a fine point on it, we spooned afterwards. No jumping up to get coffee, no laptop with videos, just enjoying the afterglow. All thoughts of Dom dematerialized. Dismissed once again as nothing but brain junk.

Eventually, sometime after noon, I got up and started the coffee. When I returned, Richard was sitting in Colleen's lap. I almost dropped the mugs.

"I know, I think the dick likes me," she said. Of all the weird things that had happened recently, this was by far the weirdest. I climbed into bed and handed her a mug, which she took mindfully so as to not disturb the cat. I could hear him purring.

"Huh…you figured out how to charm animals."

I wasn't on the schedule that night, so we had the whole afternoon and night to ourselves. A quick look around the kitchen told me that I needed to go shopping again too. A longer look around the kitchen told me cleaning wouldn't be a bad idea either. Colleen and I took care of some household chores while listening to heavy metal which made them feel much less like chores. Having a demon to help with housework is awesome. Ten out of ten would highly recommend.

We stopped by the sex shop, where the beehive lady now knew me by name, and took a look around. I was pondering some highly technically advanced vibrators, while Colleen perused the BDSM gear.

"Hey! What do you think?" Colleen had a pair of nipple clamps dangling from her breasts. She giggled and the chains attached to them jingled.

"Cute."

"Oooo, look they have butt plugs with tails on them."

"Please don't try that on in the store," but I was too late.

"You can try stuff on in the dressing…," the beehive lady started to say, thinking I was talking to her. I should really learn her name. Her sentence was cut off and she was staring at something. Well… not something, but a rainbow-colored raccoon tail floating in mid-air. Her eyes grew wide as she watched the attached metal plug appear before it dropped to the floor with a clunk. I moved quickly to pick it up while Colleen shrugged.

"Uh... I'll take this," I paused then added, "Wow, technology these days," I gave her my best *I swear you didn't see what you thought you did* smile. She followed me to the counter where she rang me up in stunned silence. I said goodbye and left.

"Well, I think we had better find another sex shop." I said to my naked sex demon after we got into the car.

"Probably not a bad idea," she said, and we both started laughing.

An hour or so later, we were home with the groceries. I made us a nice dinner, I'm tempted to say a romantic dinner, but I'm not quite ready to admit that just yet. We picked out a not rom com and settled in for the evening with a loaded pipe. The movie was starting to suck, and we started to fool around. Colleen decided I might look cute with a tail, and I don't know if I looked cute or not, but I was squealing like an animal when a knock came at the door.

A knock that was becoming familiar. I thought about ignoring it, but then I heard through the door, "Is everything ok?" Fuck.

26

I removed my tail, a little faster than I should have and threw on a robe that I was smart enough to have had handy. Colleen went into ghost mode as I opened the door.

"Are you ok? It sounded like you were in distress." Detective Shelton said. He was peering into my living room and passed my shoulder. His eyebrow raised, "Are you alone?" I turned my head and saw that he was staring at the rainbow raccoon tail butt plug that was currently resting on my rumpled sofa.

"Uh…. Yeah, I am. And I'm fine. Just doing some yoga."

"Yeah, butt yoga," Colleen giggled, unhelpfully.

The detective's eyebrow stayed raised, "Those breathing techniques are complicated." Now he was just fucking with me.

"How can I help you Detective?" I asked, not inviting him in and hoping he would take the hint.

"Good news, I wanted to tell you that I checked into the missing dancer. And she is fine. It looks like you were just missing her because she works a different shift." *Yeah, great news, now scram.* "I'm still looking into that podcast.

It's a pretty obvious con. Fairly common, not sure there is anything illegal, but I have my fraud guys looking into it. It doesn't look like it's your co-worker either. If I find anything, I'll let you know. But otherwise, I wouldn't worry about it."

"Oh yeah, that's great." I said and started to say thank you and buh bye, but he kept talking and produced a pamphlet from his jacket pocket.

"I think you should take a look at this," I took the pamphlet from him without looking at it. "And also, I wanted to let you know that we are closing the cases on both Mary and Scott. Both deaths have been ruled to be death by natural causes likely heart attacks, the customer at the club was also determined to have been a heart attack. Just an odd series of unconnected coincidences." That's what came out of his mouth, but his eyes said something different. "I have to say, that it is very strange that you have encountered so many heart attacks in such a short period of time. That must be unnerving for you." Colleen was no longer giggling and standing right behind me.

The chill caused me to inhale deeply, "Yeah, it's weird for sure. I'm glad that there's no one out there killing people." Colleen jabbed me in the left butt cheek, and I stumbled forward. "Strong draft, I need to have my AC looked at." Detective Shelton looked skeptical, which was kind of his thing.

"Well, I'll let you get back to your….yoga," he knew it wasn't yoga. "Thank you for your time and cooperation."

"You're welcome. Nice to meet you," I said despite it not being nice to meet him. "Bye!" I closed the door without letting him respond.

I looked at the sofa where Colleen was sitting, "See, I told you it was all good." I shrugged and looked at the pamphlet that Shelton had given me. It was titled "How to tell real from fake on the internet."

I tossed it to her, "I think you may need to look at this."

She looked at it and tossed it aside without looking at it, and picked up the plug by the tail, "Now where were we?" I joined her back on the sofa to continue our *yoga.*

The next evening, I returned to work and Angel was slightly less frigid. Which was becoming alarming. While I consider myself a fairly likable person, she didn't all of a sudden develop a fondness for me. Something was off. The dressing room was chillier than usual too. Colleen was there, but it wasn't her making things chilly. All the girls, even Honey, who I thought was my friend, wouldn't so much as look at me. At least not directly. I got the side eye, from everyone. All the talk was in hushed tones that I had no hope of hearing. I looked to Colleen to see if she knew what was up, but she just shrugged. She got close enough to some of the whispers presumably to hear what they were, but not close enough that she would give them goosebumps. That dark look came over her again. This time it scared me. But she gave me the look that said I would have to wait for us to be alone before she would tell me. She stayed in the dressing room while I checked in. Even Lars, not known for his small talk, didn't speak to me beyond what was absolutely essential to the job. The only person not looking at me like I was some kind of an asshole was Dom. I walked over to him at his usual place at the VIP room entrance.

"Hey Lacey," he said, making my knees weak.

"Hey," I replied. Thinking I shouldn't say anything else. Just let him talk and respond naturally and thoughtfully, thereby mitigating the chance I would say something dumb. But then I said, "I think people are mad at me. When I walked into the dressing room, they acted like I blew a rancid egg fart or something." Because when you are talking to someone as hot as the sun and hoping they might like you back, it's important to bring up rancid egg farts.

"Ha ha!" He was laughing so maybe all was not lost. Note to self, more fart jokes. "An IRS investigator came to the club yesterday. Word on the grapevine is that the dead guy in the VIP brought heat down on the club."

"And the girls think I killed that guy with a magical lap dance." Technically it was Colleen's magic lap dance.

"That's about the gist of it. I know that you didn't kill that guy. But rumors are rarely based in truth." This one kind of was though. I can't be sure it was Detective Shelton that sicced the IRS on the club, but if not, it was an uncanny coincidence. But I was more curious how Dom happened to be the only one in the club who knew that none of it was my fault. Not directly my fault anyway. Maybe he didn't and assumed that was because he really liked me. A girl can hope.

"I think it was Lexus who spread the rumors."

"Nope. Angel."

"That's why she wasn't as horrible to me the last couple of nights."

"Exactly. But you came in like a hurricane. You were bound to become a target of something nasty. It's not a kind industry."

"I'm starting to see that."

"Just keep your head down and be about your business. Sometimes this stuff just blows over. Trust me, you got enough friends." Again, with the cryptic speak.

"Well… thanks for talking to me about all this stuff."

"I got you."

I nodded and walked toward a customer who had been staring at my ass. We went into the VIP, and I gave him a not deadly dance. But I had a hard time focusing on my work, I mean he was having a hard time, but that was kind of the point. My hard time had to do with the fact that the honeymoon phase of my job had ended abruptly. I loved the freedom of my job. Independence, money, and that a bra wasn't required, but I was starting to think that it might be time to find another place to work. Dom said that this stuff would blow over, but it seemed to me that it was pretty serious. Colleen had found out that there was some shady stuff with the books, I'm pretty sure that the IRS investigator would find it too. And everyone thought that I was to blame. Kind of because I was, but that's beside the point. I had no intention of being the pariah of my workplace.

I went about my business as advised and just avoided everyone but the customers. It was middle school all over again. I was the odd man out, the interloper. The not cool one. It sucked, and to make it worse, Colleen hadn't shown back up since I left the dressing room. I assumed she was trying to find out more stuff, but I really wished she had stayed with me. Especially at the end of the night when I was leaving the mostly empty VIP room.

The VIP was a dark place tucked back in the corner of the club. It wasn't completely private, but if you were trying to corner someone and knew where all the cameras were located, or not located, it was perfect. Which is why Angel confronted me there. I said goodbye to my last very much alive customer and stopped in the short dark hallway that led to the main floor to count my money and figure out my tips. I had made a good amount of money. One of my best nights in fact, and I was totally distracted while I was reveling in that fact. Angel, who had apparently been lurking in the shadows, appeared out of nowhere. Like a ghost.

"Looks like you've done pretty well tonight," she cooed. I wondered where the hell my demon was. Or my bouncer for that matter.

"Uh, yeah. Not bad." I was trying to sound cool. Emphasis on the trying part.

"Things are getting pretty rough for you here lately. It's not going great for me either. I have my situation under control though. Yours, however, can get a lot worse." I was skeptical actually. "But I can help you. Call off the dogs, or bitches for you. I'll take half." She held out her hand, as two other girls materialized out of darkness. Two very large girls I might add.

"Um…"

"Trust me when I say, you don't know who you're fucking with. The IRS is full of a bunch of pussies and are already off my case. But this isn't about your shifts, or your job. You can quit, I don't care, but you owe me, and you're going to pay." I got the clear inference that she intended to hurt me, or her minions did. And not just with passive aggressive insults and dirty looks.

Colleen was nowhere to be found, as Angel lifted her hand directing the two girls to move closer. I had seen them around but hadn't talked to them. They didn't appear exactly approachable. And I had never seen them do a lap dance, why rub your ass on a stranger's erection when you could just steal money from the girls that did. I've never been in a fight. Ever. My bullies had been mean, but they tended to disappear before anything got physical. Sure, I love violence in movies and books and thrash metal, but I was a coward in real life. These chicks were about to kick my ass. I was alone. I handed Angel half my cash.

27

Colleen showed up as just as Dom was walking me to my car. As we drove away, we were silent. But the sense that there was something important that we both needed to say was palpable. It hung thick in the air, not unlike a rancid egg fart that no one wants to acknowledge, lest they catch the blame. In fact, Dom had been quiet also after our conversation. He only said a cool goodbye. I wanted to tell him about what Angel and her buddies had done but thought better of it. It seemed like he was on my side, but I wasn't sure if I should trust him. He was hot as hell, but that didn't mean he was a good guy. For all I knew, he could have been the one to tell her where I was and when. His post was the VIP room. It wasn't hard to see him as the good cop to set me up to get jumped by the bad cop. It would be terribly disappointing but not inconceivable. I had a hard time believing that he didn't know it was happening. That he did nothing if he did know would be indicative of him being a full-fledged douche canoe. I'm not sure I even wanted to know if that was the case or not.

I was a bit salty with Colleen for not being there either. The fact that she hadn't said anything to me since we got into the car wasn't helping. But as annoyed with her as I was for leaving me to fend for myself, I was kind of glad she wasn't there. As I suspect there would have been another death to fuel Detective Shelton's suspicions. At that point, I was cautiously optimistic that I wouldn't see him again.

Since she wasn't there to protect me, I wasn't sure that I should tell her. I knew I couldn't stop her from going after Angel. So far, she had only killed people in the act of sex dreams, that I knew of at least. I didn't know for sure if she had the capability to kill beyond that. But it seemed like a prudent assumption. She, and by proxy I, had enough blood on our hands. Shelton appeared to have fucked off for good, so I didn't see a good reason to tell her. Not that I would mind not having Angel around. Forever. Maybe one day, when Angel wasn't a factor in my life anymore, I would tell her. But for now, I thought keeping it from her was the best way to keep homicide detectives out of my life. Even if it meant that Angel would be in my life too.

In the dressing room, she looked like she couldn't wait to tell me what she had heard the girls talking about. But now that we were alone, she didn't seem as eager to tell me. It dawned on me that she might have seen me talking to Dom again and figured he told me everything. So maybe she was salty at me too. However unjustified. I felt my reason for being salty was more valid for sure. I almost got jumped for fuck's sake. Can't say I thought that would ever happen to someone who had a demon for a girlfriend. She said she was there for my protection but went missing when I needed her. Maybe I was extra salty. But I did think it was important to hear what the girls actually said, as opposed to what Dom told me. If I was skeptical of his intentions, then I needed to hear what Colleen had heard.

"So.....what were the girls talking about?" I tried to sound not salty. I don't know if I succeeded.

"Oh, that. I figured Dom told you. Not sure what you need me for." She said confirming my assumption.

"Dom told me a little, but not as much as I would have liked, I'm not sure I can totally trust him. You I trust." *Mostly.* "What did they say?" I tried to gloss over her passive aggressive jealous inference.

"They were saying that you killed the Paul VIP guy, probably to rob him, and that to throw the cops off your trail you gave them a bunch of bullshit about Angel and the books. And that the club might get shut down because of it, and it made them rally around Angel. They hate her, especially the ones that have had to pay her off, but it seems that she got them to hate you more. They think the club is in danger of being shut down. They don't want real jobs."

"Hard to blame them, really. It's a good job. If you can avoid old smelly Clyde."

"Claude, his name was Claude." Her tone was not encouraging.

"Sure. But for real, where can you find a job where people compliment you while handing you money. It's a good gig. Dom said he thinks that it might all blow over."

"I don't think he's wrong. It's not great now, but it seems to me, given what I've heard as the ghost..." *Demon.* "...in the room that drama comes and goes. The longer it goes on the less traction it gets until something else comes along to replace it." I don't think I have to say how surprised I was that she agreed with him. I would have expected her to disagree out of pure spite. I may not have given her enough credit.

"Maybe, I guess."

"Don't worry about it." Her tone was not jovial. I really hated it when she got like this, which seemed much more frequent lately.

We got home, and to my utter surprise tinged with a bit of jealousy, Richard wound himself around Colleen's legs as soon as she went solid.

"He likes you." I saltily said, while trying again not to sound salty.

"I have a way with dicks," she said. I thought for just a minute that her dark mood had passed but her tone still wasn't right. I laughed anyway.

We got ready for bed, and I waited for Colleen to start something, but she still seemed preoccupied. And when I woke up the next day, I was alone. Even Richard was missing. I heard her in the living room, tapping on the keyboard of the computer. I smelled coffee. And muffins? I listened to the sound of the keyboard and took several long deep breaths, hoping the scent of the coffee would dispel the remains of my dream. Yet another dream about Dom. It was happening nightly now. He seemed to be all I dreamed about. I really hoped that Colleen would come around about him and get over her jealously. I figured a night with him, assuming he wasn't a douche, and also assuming that he wanted to have sex with me, consent is the most important thing after all, would get him out of my system.

Finally, I threw off the covers and got up. Colleen was sitting at the dining room table with a mug of coffee and Richard in her lap. Now I was jealous. That was very much my cat.

"Good morning sunshine!" I said. She must not have sensed me come into the room because she jumped and closed the laptop abruptly. Not suspicious at all. Nope, not even a little.

"I made muffins!" she said, matching my tone. Now I was even more suspicious.

"I smelled them."

"You like the smell of my muffin?" There was the demon I knew and loved. At least a glimpse of her.

"I do." I said with an awkward wink.

"They're strawberry."

"Ooo…. Are they pink?" I tried my wink again, but I think I just blinked. She giggled anyway. I went and got coffee and a muffin, which were amaze balls. "Dude, these are great," I said through a mouthful of my girlfriend's muffin. "I didn't know you could bake."

"Me either, but I can follow a recipe. I found it online, and we had all the stuff so I thought I would surprise you. I'm sorry I was kind of a turd about Dom." That was a bigger surprise than the muffins.

"It's ok, it's flattering. He's hot as fuck. I'd rather you be jealous than leave me for him."

"I'm not going anywhere," it came out slightly more menacing than I would have liked. But I tried to appreciate the sentiment.

"What were you looking up?"

"Nothing. Recipes I told you." And there went our lovely afternoon.

"Sorry, didn't mean it like that." I totally meant it like that. She was obviously looking at something she hadn't wanted me to see. "These are really great." I said, trying to recover our conversation. It worked sort of.

I didn't plan on working, and honestly didn't want to after the night before. The chores were done, and we sat on the couch, full of strawberry muffins. Colleen put on a crime documentary, what we liked to call murder porn, and we only sort of paid attention. I packed a bowl, but Colleen said she wasn't in the mood. I was still stewing on the shit with Angel, and it didn't help that I couldn't talk to Colleen about it.

"What do think I put the house up for sale and we move somewhere far away? You could go solid all the time and we could be like a real couple?"

"Because of Angel?"

"Yeah, kind of. Work was hard last night. Honestly," I wasn't sure I should say this, but she was my girlfriend and I needed to tell her how I felt. "I really missed you last night. I felt very alone."

"I am so sorry, Lacey. But I promise, I had a good reason." She looked genuinely sorry.

"A reason you're not going to tell me?"

"I can't right now. But know this… Angel will not be a problem much longer." Her pale violet eyes glowed red. In fact, all of her glowed red. But before I could even get scared, I got very sleepy, and I guess I took a nap.

28

Colleen

I know, I looked like an ass. But I don't care. I know what happened. So did Dom. Dom and I were watching. Him in the flesh, me not so much. I never felt as much like a demon as I did when Lacey handed that hate filled twat waffle her money. I was filled with a rage that I hadn't felt since she was a kid getting bullied by the same species of twat waffles.

Did I like Dom? I wasn't sure. But I knew he cared for Lacey and so we had the same objective. To protect her. What happened after that, I wasn't sure. But while we were figuring that out, we were allies.

Dom is an incubus. A male sex demon, and an ancient one. And one that is more powerful than me. A fact I learned the hard way.

After Lacey left the dressing room, I stayed and listened for a while. But it wasn't hard to figure out what had happened there. Angel and her crap. What was hard was not simply burning the whole place to the ground.

I followed her out to the floor. She was not alone the whole night. Not at all. I was with her the whole time. So was Dom. As much as I would like him to be a douche canoe, he just isn't. I heard their conversation, and he told her the truth. What he didn't tell her is that he has known about me all along. Nor did he tell her that she is his new favorite human. After she walked away to go work, he looked at me and winked. Imagine my surprise. You don't have to imagine actually, I'm about to tell you. I was shocked. Shocked I tell you. Other than Lacey, or other humans when I go solid, no one has seen me. Or at least they have had the sense not to let me know they have.

He spoke quietly, so that no one else heard him talking to, well no one. He told me what he was. He also told me that it was time for Angel to go. He was done letting her run her bullshit. She had done enough damage. When I asked him what made him decide now was the time, given that she had already caused so much grief, his answer was Lacey. So now you understand the salt. I had good reason for being jealous. But like I said, he is more powerful than I am. By a lot.

My first reaction was to try to put him to sleep. Right there in the middle of the floor. He actually laughed at me. Then for only a split second, his deep dark eyes glowed red. Which is actually pretty cool. And you may have noticed, I can do that too. Anyway, when that failed, I tried simply to punch him in his unbelievably handsome face. But my fist simply stopped short. I was completely unable to move it until I promised him I would stop. So, I did.

That's when we became allies, if not friends.

After Lacey went to bed, I met up with Dom at his house. We started planning Angel's demise. Yes, an actual, technical murder. I'm a demon, remember. While I do feel some remorse for my accidental deaths, I feel exactly none for Angel's. Why? Because fuck her, that's why. He knew everything about her. He's a researcher, like me. We planned for the next day. It had to be daytime because Angel was at the club most nights. We didn't want there to be any way that it could be tied to Lacey. That was really the most important thing. That and that Angel die screaming. That was important too.

Dom told me that Angel sleeps late, but in the afternoons, before work, she liked to go to the park and feed the birds. I know you want to feel sorry for her, but don't. She was nice to birds, so what? She took who knows how much money from innocent women. Mostly innocent. But still. Even if she wasn't a murderer, or a grifting podcaster, she was still a rotten person. The park was a public place and was the most logical place for Angel to meet her fate. Lacey would be safely napping at home, and nowhere near it. We wanted it to make the news. That way, there wouldn't be any hint, not even a suggestion that it could be connected to her. The last thing I wanted was any reason at all for Detective Shelton to come back, that guy had the worst timing ever.

I wasn't with Dom very long, just long enough to plan our revenge. But in the course of our collusion, he started to grow on me. I was still jealous, but much to my disappointment, I had to admit he wasn't a douche. I didn't actually want to leave, as he was the first of my kind that I had met. I learned so much about myself on my own, but I still had a few questions that I thought he might be able to answer. As soon as our plan was in place, I went back to Lacey's. My questions would have to wait.

After I put Lacey to sleep, kind of a dick move, but necessary, I met Dom in the park. Angel wasn't there yet. We waited and watched the old people in the park. Mostly they just sat on the benches reading old paperbacks and newspapers. I felt bad about what they were about to witness. But we needed witnesses, and this was the best time to do it. When there were just old people and not a bunch of kids. And I felt better about traumatizing old people than kids.

While we were waiting for the leader of the illmuniTwati to show up, as Dom promised she would, I asked him a few things. Like how the red eye thing worked. He explained that you had to be really angry, and it would just happen. I suppose I hadn't been that mad before. Most of the people, or all of the people I had accidentally killed, had been when I was horny not mad. I was about to ask him how I could get semen without killing, but Angel showed up before I could. It was show time. But the more time we spent talking, the more I started to like him. Albeit reluctantly.

Angel was wearing a sundress. An ugly one, if I may add. It was purple with white polka dots. Hideous. That alone could have been reason enough to kill her. Just kidding. Sort of. She had headphones on and was lip syncing to the lyrics of some song. Taylor Swift, I thought it sounded like, but I wasn't sure, as I've never actually listened to that kind of stuff deliberately. Angel walked to a bench under a tree and sat down. The pigeons must have recognized her because as soon she sat down, they gathered around her. She dropped handfuls of birdseed. Bird seed she probably bought with my Lacey's money. I felt my eyes glow red. Dom and I let them eat, they would need their strength.

I've heard pigeons described as flying rats, which I don't get. They seem like nice birds. Sure, they eat garbage and shit on everything, but hell, we found Richard eating out of the garbage. Although, he was more discerning about where he shat. He was fastidious about using the litter box. When they looked like they had plenty of bird seed, Dom opened his utterly glorious glossy black wings. I could see why Lacey wanted to do him so badly. I did the same with my own. It felt really good, I had never shown my wings to Lacey. I thought it might scare her too badly. He reached to the sky with his equally magnificent, muscled arms, arms I might like to have wrapped around me. Did I mention he was naked?

Let me try again, he reached to the sky and then brought his arms down like he was conducting an orchestra. In a way, he was. I copied him again. The pigeons all flew up and swarmed Angel. Screeching and squawking, they attacked her. She began to scream. They pecked at her and tore at her skin. Taking chunks of flesh with them as they flew away and then came back for seconds. The blood ran down the bench. Her headphones dropped to the ground as one of the birds flew away with her ear and I could hear the music she was listening to. It *was* Taylor Swift by the way. I wondered if the birds would be enough to actually kill her but stopped wondering when I saw a loop of her intestines land in a pile of bird seed. At least I'm pretty sure it was intestine. I'll admit, I have yet to research human biology.

Angel would trouble no stripper ever again. The pigeons began to disperse, having left behind a large pile of red glistening flesh, a part of her purple dress still remained. One of the more technically savvy old men had taken video of the whole thing with his phone. With Lacey nowhere to be found. Well, you could find her on the couch actually, which was nowhere near the crime scene. Or freak accident scene. It was perfect. A random pigeon attack. I wasn't sure how much I had actually contributed though, having never tried to command a flock of birds before. Or any animal for that matter. My revenge felt incomplete. So I focused my attention on a lone robin I saw sitting in the tree above the bench. The robin came down from the tree. An eyeball floated in the pile of flesh and bones that had been the horrible, no good, rotten door girl, the robin plucked it out of the mess and flew away with it. I felt like a proper helper then.

So, I guess I am technically a murderer. But am I really though? It was Dom that mostly conducted the birds, even if they were my idea. So maybe just a coconspirator. I'm really only guilty of some mild postmortem mutilation. Not to mention Angel did like feeding the birds, so maybe it's what she would have wanted. Part of her will always be with them, so she's in a better place too. I'm not all bad.

29

I awoke on the couch to a smiling demon. I was absolutely terrified. Not hurt or just scared, but terrified. I backed away from her but didn't get past the arm of the sofa. The last thing I remember before passing out was her eyes. Those red eyes. If I harbored any doubt at all that she was a demon, it was wiped out in that moment. I was afraid of her, even more so as she smiled at me like nothing had happened.

"Get away from me," I managed to get out, but then became even more frightened because I wondered if that might provoke her further. I had no clue why she put me to sleep or what she had done while I was out. Not to mention, the only other time she had put me to sleep, I'm pretty sure it was to dismember somebody.

"No. It's okay. I promise. I won't hurt you. Not ever. No matter what." She seemed sincere, but she was a fucking demon. What kind of an idiot was I to trust a demon?

"Why did you do that?"

"I had to. Please don't be mad. Or scared." I had never heard her beg before, but that's what she was doing now. Begging. I almost felt sorry for her. But those eyes. Those beautiful eyes, full of pure hatred. She was evil incarnate. She moved to hug me, but I backed away again. This time up and over the back of the arm and on to the floor. Richard came and licked my face. Oblivious to the demon in the room.

"Will you just go? Leave me alone. I don't want you here anymore." I figured, either she would kill me, or listen and leave. She did neither.

"I love you, Lacey. Please don't make me leave." I didn't actually know that I could make her leave.

"No. This is over Colleen." Then the weirdest thing happened, she left. Simply dematerialized. But not before the tears in her eyes broke my heart.

Richard began to howl. Like I'd never heard him do before. It was as if I had thrown him out too. I wondered if she was still there, just invisible to me. But the way the cat was howling and looking around made me think that she had actually left. She was really gone. I missed her instantly. Like when you let your hairdresser lop off too much hair and instantly regret it. I was confused and frightened. And I felt really stupid. Was she really evil? Should I have let her explain more, or just trusted her? She had never hurt me before, and she left when I asked her to. I was shaking. I began to cry.

Richard seemed to be in distress, but sensed I was too. He climbed up on my lap after I had repositioned myself on the sofa. I reached for the pipe and tried to take a hit, but I was sobbing much too hard. Even if I had been under her spell, the heartache was real. She had scared me, but I still wondered how I would go on without her. She had been my everything. This naïvely inquisitive horny sex demon. The person, or not person, whom I had spent the last three years with. Maybe the best years of my life. And now she was gone.

I don't know how long I sat there and cried. Richard was nearly soaked with my tears, but he didn't seem to mind. My dumpster cat was all I had left in the world. I petted his head, and he purred softly. I was so grateful that I wasn't on the schedule that night. Tomorrow night would suck, but at least I had a night to get my shit together.

I mulled around my house, trying to get rid of things that reminded me of her. Bert and Ernie went into the trash. As did the rainbow tail butt plug. I guess the one good thing about breaking up with demon is that there were no photos to delete or crop her face out of. Richard kept searching for her, and that didn't help at all. It was still a mystery why he got attached to her when he had hated her so much. Since she had named him, it occurred to me that I might want to change his name. But he seemed to know it, and that seemed like a dick move on my part. It wasn't his fault a demon gave him his name.

At some point, close to dawn, I crawled in bed and went to sleep. Sort of. I tossed and turned and dreamed of demons. Not the sexy kind with a knack for cunnilingus, but the scary kind. The ones with horns, sharp teeth, and huge wings. Blood and gore, and for some odd reason, pigeons haunted me as I slept.

When I woke, tangled in sweat covered sheets, sometime in the early afternoon, Richard was lying on Colleen's pillow. Something of hers I had forgotten to throw away. I rolled over to pet him and her scent rose up from the pillow. I burst into tears again. When I was able to stop crying, I got up to make the coffee and feed my cat. I wanted, needed to continue with some sort of routine. I took my coffee back to bed.

I had a TV in my bedroom, but almost never turned it on. The last few years, I had coffee in bed with Colleen. We either talked or watched videos on the computer but had not really watched TV in there. We had always found other ways to occupy ourselves. But now that I was alone, I turned it on. I wanted something mindless to take my mind off of her, so that I might be able to keep it together to go to work. I tuned into a soap opera. Which was so bad that it succeeded in distracting me at least temporarily.

I began to seriously consider selling the house and moving. Not that I could hide from her. If she wanted to find me, I had no doubt that she would. I got up and sat at the dining room table, when I booted up the computer, the page that Colleen hadn't wanted me to see was still up. Something about incubi. The muffin recipe was still open too. I clicked bookmark on that one, because the muffins had really been that good. It struck me as odd that she had not wanted me to see the other page though. Why would she have not wanted me to see that she was trying to learn about her male counterpart. A thought began to rise from the recesses of my mind, but slithered away when I tried to get a grasp on it. I almost started crying again but was able to hold it back.

I began to look for places I might like to live. I didn't like the idea of selling mom's house, but I needed a fresh start. Angel had kind of fucked up my job, but I didn't think it would be hard to find a strip club to work in. I would have to go back until the house sold and to make enough money to be able to move, but I thought I could manage. Head down and just be about my business, like Dom had said.

I looked at places on the east coast, Boston looked kind of cool. Then I considered Vegas, but there seemed like way too many people there. The southern states didn't look cool at all. Alligators and humidity were a deal breaker for sure. In the end, I saved a few places, but didn't make any kind of a decision at all. I decided I would pick it up tomorrow.

I jumped in the shower to get ready for work, but when I got out, I saw that I had a text from Rick. He said not to come in because the club was going to be closed for a few days. I thought it was weird, but I was relieved. Some sort of maintenance issue I assumed. I wasn't sure if I could make it through the night without crying while lap dancing anyway. No guy wants a crying stripper. Well... there's probably one or two that do. There really is a kink for everything. Some more benevolent than others.

I made myself some dinner and settled in for my second night alone. I turned on the TV while I ate. The news was on, and I didn't bother to change the station. I couldn't remember the last time I had actually watched the evening news. Occasionally, I checked my news app, and my phone always informed me of the weather forecast. I rarely catch the local news. There was something about a lady getting killed in the park. I turned the channel. Probably a jogger or something. I wanted something a bit more uplifting. I found an old episode of *Friends* and tried to watch that. That made me feel much worse, so I found some murder porn. Not uplifting, in the slightest, but worked while I ate. And the narrator was kind of soothing.

I woke up on the couch the next day. TV still on, my dinner plate still on the coffee table, with Richard snuggled up by my feet. The next couple of days passed pretty much like that. No sign of Colleen, Richard my only companion, as I wallowed in sorrow and self-pity.

30

The club reopened on a Thursday. Somehow, I put myself together and dragged my ass to work. As I got out of my car, I prepared for the snarling Angel. More determined than ever to find another job. Although, if I had to keep giving her half my money, it would take twice as long to move. As I shut my car door, I wondered if I should try and find a sugar daddy. Just long enough to get out of there and start fresh. Of course, I could always get a real job. But that seemed worse than putting up with Angel or a dirty old man. Especially if it were only temporary.

I pulled open the heavy door to the club, and the smell of ancient cigarette smoke and night musk body spray hit me. If they had been closed for maintenance, it hadn't been for fresh paint and new carpeting. Jess was sitting in Angel's spot. I had only met her once, on the Sunday Rick called me in to work. She didn't seem to notice my surprise to see her there in Angel's place. My pleasant surprise, I should add. I thought about asking where Angel was, but then remembered that I didn't care. And I didn't want to jinx the only positive thing to happen in the last few days.

"Hello," I said. She smiled and nodded kind of somberly but didn't say anything. It was weird, but once again, I wasn't trying to jinx anything. I dropped a tip in her jar and returned her smile. I came to the DJ booth and saw Lars, but he didn't notice me. I walked by without saying hello. I headed into the dressing room, to see several girls crying lightly. I figured they all still hated me and would for a while. I didn't say anything and took my spot at a table to get ready. There was a healthy set of customers on the floor, so I focused on getting ready so I could entertain them and plan my exit strategy.

I was slathering on some lip gloss when Honey came over. I braced myself for some shit talking.

"Hey, did you hear?" She said.

I wondered if it was some kind of a trap, but thought I still needed to respond, "I don't think I did."

"Angel is dead."

I dropped my lip gloss.

"What?" was all I could say.

"She was killed a few days ago. Didn't you see the news?"

"I don't really watch the news."

"She was killed in the park," Honey said.

"Oh, I did see something about someone getting killed in the park, but I turned the channel. Was she jogging?" As it came out of my mouth, I realized that I couldn't picture Angel jogging.

The other girls, who had been crying, started to giggle. Which even *I* thought was inappropriate.

"Pigeons, she was killed by pigeons," Jasmine said, and the whole room burst into laughter. They had just been crying. Although I could see how death by pigeon might be funny. I must have looked perplexed, mostly because I was.

"Good fucking riddance," the redhead who had consoled me after barfing said. She was wearing the chain outfit again. She had not been crying by the way. "You didn't think they were crying for Angel, did you?"

"Uh, yeah. Kinda," I still looked perplexed.

"We are crying because we're relieved. Do you have any idea what kind of horrendous bullshit she made us deal with?" Honey said. I did know in fact. "She made us pay her to keep our shifts. Rick fired the two girls that helped her do it too." That was definitely good news.

"They never got shit from me," the redhead said. I believed her. She didn't look like someone anyone would want to fuck with.

"But she did me," Taylor said walking out of the small dressing room bathroom. "Dayshift sucks ass unless you have regulars. It's so slow, I barely made my rent." I almost told her I thought she was dead but thought better of it.

"She took some of my money too," I said, hoping that a relatable experience might help improve my standing with the other girls. An attempt at peopling better.

"That sucks," Honey said. "We heard about that actually."

"Um, you did? How?"

"Dom told us," Jasmine piped up. Great. So, he was in on it. I was crushed. But maybe not all that surprised. A guy that hot was bound to be a douche canoe.

"Rick told us that you didn't have anything to do with the dead guy or the IRS too by the way. I guess he had heard what everyone was saying," Honey said, like she hadn't bought into the rumors and treated me like shit too. "He said that Angel had just fucked up a form or something and that it was no big deal. And also, that the cops said the dead VIP guy died of a heart attack. Probably because I taught you to give such great lap dances." She winked, I frowned. "No one really thought you killed the guy." Awesome, so they just used that as an excuse to treat me like garbage.

"Wow. Well, I don't want to say I'm glad…"

The redhead cut me off, "You can be glad, that chick was a real cunt."

"Um ok," not that I wasn't glad, but it seemed weird to be open about it. "Pigeons though." The girls started to laugh again, and despite my best efforts at some measure of decorum, I did too. I'm sure I should have felt bad about it, but just didn't. Angel just kind of made the world a shittier place. It wasn't hard to see how everyone, especially the club, would be better off without her.

I finished getting ready and checked in with Lars, who if not apologetic was his usual grumpy self. I was so relieved.

"Hey there lady, you ready to make some boners and break some hearts?" I said I was.

The mood on the floor and the rest of the club was like a dark cloud had lifted. I ran into Lexus, and she didn't give me a dirty look. I wasn't expecting her to eat any crow, pun totally intended, and apologize. She just wasn't the type. I was satisfied with being ignored.

I avoided Dom though. Because fuck him. He must have known and let Angel take my money. I can't say that I was hurt, just incredibly disappointed. And it made him slightly less attractive. Not totally though. Normally when a hot guy turns out to be an ass, he's no longer hot. Dom was so hot though that the guy could fart in my cheerios and still be hot. Like freak of nature hot. But still, fuck him. Figuratively. Unless he apologizes.

My first night without her went better than I expected it to. I was busy all night. There was a software convention in town, and the clientele was excited to be anywhere but the hotel. Lots of brainiacs and awkward guys who were, let's say, very enthusiastic to be hanging around a bunch of naked females. I don't know how many I talked to, but none of them turned me down. My stages were all full too.

I hadn't had a night like this since my first one. But this time it was all on my own. I'll admit, I was still pretty bummed, but for a little while I forgot all about it.

I think everyone had a good night, and it was pretty obvious that the lack of Angel's oppressive presence had something to do with it. The good vibes were palpable. Even the staff didn't try and hide their relief. Rick seemed the most jubilant. It was simply awesome to have her gone, there were still a few things that struck me as odd. Especially when I considered the altar thing that Colleen had said she had found in the office. That implied some sort of worship, and if that was the case, I would think there would be more people mourning instead of celebrating.

I headed to the dressing room after my last dance, which had been for a guy who had talked way too much about his video games. Nice guy, but I was ready to go home to my far less talkative cat. Since becoming a stripper, my people skills have greatly improved. Or at least my ability to fake them had. But I was never going to be a social butterfly. Faking it would be the best I would be able to achieve, and I was cool with that. My retirement plan was to collect cats and spend my golden years buried in pot smoke. That plan didn't require any people skills at all.

The girls in the dressing room were all still smiling and laughing and giggling. I decided then, that even if I were to remain mostly anti-social, I didn't want to be the kind of person that made people rejoice after I was dead. That thought made me miss Colleen though.

There were two bouncers that night, and so far, I had been able to avoid Dom. I gave him a curt nod as I walked in and out of the VIP but did not stop to talk to him. I had been hoping that the other guy, a large bald dude with a beard that hung down to his chest named Marty, would walk me out. But that was not the case, as he was busy walking out other girls. I let Dom take my bag but kept quiet. I tried not to look at him. He put my stuff on the passenger seat and was I about to close my door after handing him his tip, but he placed his strong, large, and girthy fingers in the door jam. Rather than smash his hand by closing the door, I looked up at him with what I hoped was a dirty look and got caught in his eyes.

"I told you it would all blow over. She won't bother you or anyone else again," he said, and a red spark flickered his unbelievably beautiful eyes. I knew then why Colleen had been looking at that page. I also knew why she had put me to sleep. Pigeons of all fucking things. That was definitely Colleen.

31

Colleen

Never in a million years would I have thought Lacey could be afraid of me. I thought she understood that I was *her* demon. I could never hurt her. Well, I'm sure I could, but would never want to. Not ever. But I couldn't convince her of that. I've seen her angry and upset, but never that scared. The only reason I left was because I didn't know how else to stop her fear. I really did leave, but I didn't know where to go. She's all I've ever known. Literally. I guess I could have stayed invisible to her, but I felt like I had already caused her so much distress. I didn't want to cause any more by staying, even if she couldn't see me. She would still be able to feel me.

I thought about going to Dom's but didn't. Now that Lacey didn't want me, I thought he might swoop in to take my place. And it was hard to blame him. Lacey was a pretty sweet piece of ass. The rest of her was pretty cool too. So, I went to the club. The days that it was closed were agonizing. I knocked around the empty place like a ghost. But when it opened again it didn't get much more exciting. In case you thought that the girls were being dramatic about how bad day shift can be, I can promise you they were not. It really is that bad. Worse maybe. There were times when there was no one there at all. Like they stopped the stages until a customer came in. The few guys that did come in were all waiting for the few girls that regularly worked those shifts. Unless you were one of those girls, day shifts are just a gamble. I was bored to death.

The owner was there during the day shift. He might have been the only person to actually have been upset. I think he really liked Angel. Or he really liked being able to fuck the chick who was facilitating his questionable financial practices. I'm not sure if he was upset that she was dead or upset that he needed to find another shady bookkeeper. There was no denying that she was an excellent cooker of books, a master chef in fact.

I learned too what that altar was that I had found on my first round of snooping. Exactly nothing. Just a funky collection of old stuff that if viewed in a certain way, looked like it could have been an altar. That cabinet hadn't been opened in years, and I watched as the day manager opened it up and swept all of it into the garbage can, including that old picture of Angel.

I could hardly wait for the night shift. Mostly because I would get to see Lacey again. I stayed far enough away that she wouldn't catch a chill, but I was with her the whole time. And yeah, I might have had something to do with how well she did. But she wouldn't know that. I could tell she was bummed though. I almost let her know, but I didn't want to upset her any more than I already had. Or scare her again.

I talked to Dom again and was relieved to find he hadn't gone to Lacey. At least not yet. He was the only other being who even knew I existed. Even if he had intentions of taking my Lacey, I didn't have anyone else to talk to. And I had no idea what I was going to do.

"Hey! I really need to talk to you." I said, perhaps a bit too aggressively, as he stood at the VIP room entrance.

"Yeah, I'm sure. But we can't talk here. Meet me in my car after the club closes." He said, and I was disappointed, but I got it. He was in *human* mode. Frankly, I was impressed that he was able to pass like that full time. It was really weird for me. But I respected what he said and waited until the club closed. After Lacey went home, I slipped into his car. He didn't acknowledge my presence until we drove out of the parking lot. He was really good at being human.

"So, I guess you're coming home with me?"

"That seems to be the case."

"What about Lacey?" He asked, for some reason I thought he would know, but he didn't.

"She was really upset with me when I woke her up after that stuff with Angel. Not upset, but afraid of me. She's never been afraid of me. So, I left."

"Humans scare easily."

"I think I may have done the red eye thing, but I didn't mean to. I was really pissed about Angel taking her money."

"The glowing red eye thing will do it. But it can be very hard to control. Are you hungry?" I thought that was the weirdest thing to ask. I was a demon, why the hell would I be hungry? Unless it was for cum, I guess. I was always hungry for that. I thought maybe that's what he meant. "For cum?"

He laughed, "Well always, but being in human form will make you need real food."

"Huh, I've always eaten when I was alone with Lacey. But didn't think I had too. I just did it to be with her." At that point I wondered I how many holes I may have had in my research. "I like pizza. With pineapple like Lacey does."

"Well, for fuck's sake, don't tell anyone that. They'll know you're a demon." He laughed again, even his laugh was sexy. "I don't think I have any pizza at home. But we can pick something up. I need to eat, and then we can talk. I think there's probably a lot of stuff you need to know."

"I learned a lot from the internet!"

"Yeah, that's what I'm afraid of."

We got some burgers from a drive through and went back to his place. Which was fabulous by the way. I was too preoccupied to look around when we were planning Angel's demise. A huge house in the suburbs. Like huge. Vaulted ceilings and minimalist décor. Not anything like Lacey's humble little place. I wondered if he would let me stay here, but what I really wanted was to know if he could help me get back to her. I had gotten over my jealousy, mostly, if only because he was here with me and not her. He could have gone home with her. He hadn't said so, but I got the impression that there was an unspoken demon etiquette about not taking another demon's human. Kind of like not talking to another dancer's regular was a rule in the strip club.

We ate in his kitchen, and I ate to be polite. I hadn't been hungry. At least not for food. The more time I spent with Dom, I was becoming ravenously hungry for the other thing. But we needed to talk, and I didn't want to kill him.

"Do you think I have any chance of being with Lacey again?" I asked, but what I really wanted to know was if he had any plans to be with her himself.

"Maybe, but it has to be her choice. And if you're wondering if I am going to try and take her, you can stop now. I do like her and would love to be with her, but there is a demon code."

"I wouldn't want to unless it was her choice. I wouldn't want to use my powers of influence on her like that."

"Well, that's a good thing, because you don't have those powers."

"Wait what? I thought I could influence people?"

"Lust maybe, but not love. She did that all on her own. You are gifted with the power of seduction, but that's about as far as it goes." He said. "And it seems to me that she really loved you. I mean, she stayed after she knew what you really are." My heart, if I had one, soared.

"If I can't influence people, then all those guys at the club really liked Lacey? That wasn't me?"

"Nope. All her." Lacey would be pleased to know that. But that also meant that I hadn't killed her childhood bully Vivian. She had gotten herpes and squished by a bus all on her own. I knew I wasn't a bad demon.

"But what about the animals?"

"Animals are different. Less complicated than humans. They sense us and know we aren't human but will warm up to us if we aren't a threat. And in some cases, like with the birds, we can control them for a little while. But no matter what, we can't override free will in humans or animals." And that explains Richard. The Dick just had to warm up to me. And the pigeons apparently were more than willing to pick apart Angel on their own.

"Well, that is good to know. One thing that has been bugging me, is how do I collect semen without killing the source?"

"What do you mean? You just don't kill them."

"Umm…."

"Have you killed everyone you've fed on?"

I cringed, "Maybe." Definitely.

"So, don't do that anymore. You can get what you want without completely draining them. Humans can be ethically sourced." He raised an eyebrow critically.

"My bad."

"Yeah, your bad." He rolled his sexy eyes.

32

Dom it appears, was an incubus. How I ended up close to two sex demons is a mystery to me. Either there are more sex demons in circulation than I knew about, or I just happened to attract them. The latter is kind of a flattering thought, so I'm going to go with that. I wasn't totally sure that's what he was, but I was at like ninety-nine percent. Seriously, if you could just see him, you'd know. He had that not quite human feel like Colleen did, but I guess I hadn't really noticed it. Maybe because he was introduced to me as a human. A crazy otherworldly hot human.

Even as hot as he was, and how crazy horny dreaming about him made me, I really wanted Colleen. Demon or not. She was a killer, but an incidental one if you don't count Angel. And people and relationships grow, I bet she could change. Become just a little less murdery and a little more cum dumpstery.

But I didn't know how to contact her. I thought about getting out the Ouija board again, I hadn't used it since the first night, but she told me that was just an excuse for her to come through. I walked around my house looking for cold drafts, and found plenty in the old place, but they weren't her. I opened my computer to see if some of those fancy gadgets that the ghosthunters use might help, but it didn't take me long to see that those were full of as much shit as the Ouija board. The sun was coming up, and I had no idea where my demon was. Richard snuggled up next to me and I cried myself to sleep. I dreamt of demons, but this time the good kind. Relatively speaking.

I woke not to coffee, but to pussy on my face. Richard, and for just a split second I wondered if he was trying to suffocate me. I rolled out of bed and made some coffee and filled his dish. They say it takes about twenty minutes from your first sip of coffee for you to actually feel the caffeine, but I had an epiphany just after it touched my lips.

Dom.

Colleen knew of no one else in the world. I knew she was jealous of him, and now I knew probably for good reason, but that was where she had gone. I was sure of it. The only problem was that I didn't know how to get a hold of him. I did know how to get a hold of Rick the manager, and he would surely have Dom's phone number. I texted him. I thought about using an excuse as to why I might need his number but couldn't think of one. So, I just asked for it. And only a few seconds later, I had it.

Now do I call or text him? I didn't want to call and risk irritating him, who likes a phone call anymore? So, I decided to send a text. I typed, *Hey, I noticed that you're an incubus, any chance you know where my succubus is?* Then deleted it. Then started again, *Hey, this is Lacey.* Shit, did he even know my real name? Delete. *Lilith. I'm looking for a friend of mine and thought you might know where she is.* I stared at it for a few solid minutes, then thought *fuck it* and hit send. What is the worst thing that could happen?

He responded in seconds. "She's with me, can we come over?" So not the worst thing, or was it? Nope, I wanted her back. I responded with a simple yes.

I looked at my house, which stank of loneliness, self-pity, and cat box. I needed to rethink my retirement plan. I gathered the takeout boxes and dirty socks and deposited them where they belonged. Richard watched triumphantly as I cleaned his litter box. I didn't know how long it would take them to get there, but I looked like I had just crawled out of bed with my cat. I jumped in the shower, put on my favorite panties, and was pulling on a small tight T-shirt when there was a knock at the door. I didn't bother with the pants. I had two sex demons at the door, for fuck's sake. I didn't need pants. I pulled the door open with gusto, and my heart dropped into my panties.

Detective Shelton. His smile chased my own from my face.

"Hello, Lacey."

"Uh… Hi?" I said lamely.

"Turns out I have a few more questions."

"Ok, can we make it quick though?" I didn't know what he could possibly want, but I wasn't going to let it take long. "You caught me at a really bad time," as usual. "I have company coming."

He looked down at my bare midriff and legs, "Ok, well then, did you happen to stay at a bed and breakfast up in gold country recently?"

Fuck.

I opened my mouth to say something, when I saw Dom's car pull up behind the unmarked police vehicle. My mouth hung open as Dom got out alone and walked up behind the detective. Shelton's eyes went glassy, and Dom caught him as he fell backward. I stepped out of the doorway to allow Dom to carry him to the sofa inside. Just after I shut the door, Colleen oozed through it.

"Lacey!" Colleen was solid in an instant and wrapped her arms around me, and then her wings. Which I hadn't seen before. "I missed you! Are you still mad at me?" I hugged her back.

"No. I was miserable without you." I said.

I heard the cop grunt on my couch and looked over to see Dom staring at us wearing a grin.

"I promise I won't kill anyone again. I swear!" Colleen hugged me tighter, but then she looked at the sleeping detective and she let me go. "Well, maybe just one more time."

"No!" Dom boomed, and I was simultaneously frightened and turned on. "You ladies are going to need some guidance here." He rolled his eyes. "Colleen, I am going to need you to do exactly as I say. Can you handle that?"

She saluted enthusiastically, "Yes Sir!" She was naked with her wings spread open. I should have been terrified. But no. I knew that Dom was on my side. On her side too. And maybe it wasn't the smartest thing in the world, but I trusted him.

"Before you wake him, you'll need to go human. And you're going to seduce him." Dom said.

"Yay!" Colleen said. She was already in human form but grinning like a horny demon.

"But you're not going to kill him. Just fuck him. Got it?"

Her grin turned into a frown, "But then how to I get him to leave my Lacey alone?"

"Trust me, sex alone is enough to scramble a guy's brain. That and maybe a bit of blackmail. We get a picture or two of him between you and his homicide suspect and that will be the end of his inquiry." I looked at Dom skeptically, "You don't have to do anything Lacey, just get into a picture or two." My look didn't change.

"But what if Colleen doesn't want to?" I knew that was a stupid question the second it came out of my mouth. Colleen was already undoing his pants with gusto.

"I'm good!" She said with Detective Shelton's belt between her teeth.

I regretted thinking that Dom had been a douche before. Maybe it was a little douchey that he hadn't stepped in with Angel, but he had still been looking out for me. The whole club really. So not quite a douche. And his ideas, at least so far, had been much better than Colleen's.

We left the detective sleeping, while Colleen had her way. I posed for a few pictures, which Dom took on the cop's and my phone. I took a look in his notebook and saw that he knew I had been in town when Alex disappeared. I shuddered when I saw that they had found traces of blood on a saw in the basement of the bed and breakfast, but they didn't find the body. Or parts. There was still nothing to tie it to me. No one saw him go to our room. So just another unfortunate coincidence.

I heard the cop grunt as I closed his notebook and looked over just in time to see Colleen lick her lips. She looked down in horror, but then smiled when she saw that he was still breathing.

"I did it!" she said with all the pride of a kid who had just completed their first successful cartwheel. "He's not dead!"

"Great!" I looked at Dom, "Now what?"

"We wake him and let him figure stuff out. He's a smart guy. I don't think we'll have to do much. I'm going ghost."

Dom dematerialized and gave two thumbs up. Colleen put her hand on Detective Shelton but stayed solid. I was still in my shirt and panties. He could come to the club if he wanted to see my tits. His eyelids fluttered and opened slowly. But shot open when he saw Colleen. He sat up on the sofa and realized he was naked. He gasped and scooted backward, over the arm and landed on the floor with a thud. I knew the feeling.

"What happened?" he croaked, still wide-eyed.

"I did," Colleen said smirking.

I almost said something but caught myself in time. I could only fuck this up, the less I said the better. I handed him his phone with his photo gallery open. He stared at it for a moment, then hit the delete button. Without speaking, I held up my own phone so he could see the duplicate pictures. In a frenetic panic, he began to gather his clothes and dress himself. Colleen handed him his belt with a demonic smile.

As he opened the door, he said, "I was never here."

"Nope, never saw you," I said as I waved goodbye.

33

After I shut the door, I turned toward my living room. There stood two of the most unimaginably beautiful beings. Well, sex demons. Dom stood naked with his wings spread. He looked like a painting, each muscle defined and glistening, his wings framing his body, and his perfectly sculpted face wore a look of seduction that made me ache. Colleen next to him, in all her pale contrast. Her body stood in stark relief from her black wings, her hair swept to one side in the front of her laid against a perfect breast. She didn't have the same seductive look as Dom. Instead, her eyes reflected that curious innocence and pure lust that I had fallen in love with. I wanted to strip and give in to both of them right there. But I held back.

I wanted to test my will. I wanted them more than anything else in the whole world then, but I needed to know how much of that need came from them, or me. Were they manipulating a simple human, leaving me with only the illusion of choice? Or was this what I really wanted? I only knew of their kind from what Colleen had told me, and considering all that had happened, I wasn't sure I entirely trusted her researching skills. I needed to know how much control I really had over my own body and mind. I needed to know if I could resist. There were a ton of other things that I needed to know also. And it seemed that Dom might have more answers than Colleen.

"Wow, guys that's quite the display," I said lamely, my panties had become uncomfortable.

"You can have us both," Dom said, making my aching resistance much worse. My eyes drifted downward to the otherworldly member that rested between his thighs. My nipples stiffened. Colleen's did too as she gave me that look from under her eyelashes. Richard strode into the room and began to coil himself around first Colleen's legs and then Dom's.

I took a deep breath and strengthened my resolve, "This has been a long, dark, hard…." My eyes drifted to the demon penis again, "Uh…strange and confusing trip." I began to quiver, "But there are some things I need to know, before we..." Richard hopped up into Colleen's arms and she stroked his head.

Dom folded his wings, and in an instant was back in human form. Fully clothed, to my utter disappointment. Colleen looked over at him, apparently disappointed too. But followed suit, understanding his intentions. She went into human form. Rather than her usual outfit, she had donned a pink bunny onesie, in what I think was an attempt to not look sexy. She failed miserably. Richard stayed snuggled in her arms.

I realized that I had been holding my breath and let it out, the ache in my crotch seemed to have lessened slightly too. My thoughts were marginally clearer, although I was still terribly preoccupied with the vision of an unholy threesome. I wonder if there is such a thing as a holy threesome. Dom and Colleen, still holding my cat, took seats on the sofa. I joined them, thinking I had proved I possessed the willpower to resist, not just one incredibly hot cum demon, but two. And they had respected my wishes for answers. It was too bad that all those questions had escaped my mind as they stood there naked.

"Please Lacey, ask what you need to know." Dom said.

I giggled, "I can't remember now." A stupid thing to say, but I felt like I had passed that point where it mattered.

"Ok, well, how about I start with me?" he said, and I nodded yes. "I have been here over a hundred years now. I came to a young lady, who was in despair. I have no memories before that, only darkness. I stayed with her until her death. After she died, I was drawn to another and stayed with her until she passed away ten years ago. It was then that I decided to live as a human. I found work in the strip club hoping that I would find another love."

Colleen hung on his every word, "How did you know you were an incubus?"

"My first was a historian and mythical expert. She taught me who I was and helped me to grow and move undetected around humans."

"A researcher!" Colleen said.

"No, an expert. A real expert." He said, and Colleen rolled her eyes.

"So, you've never accidentally killed anyone?" I asked, glancing at Colleen.

"No, not accidentally," he said. I wasn't sure if I wanted him to elaborate, but then he did. "Angel was not my first kill. But the only other life I have taken was a direct threat to my human."

"Technically the pigeons killed her," Colleen interjected. "We can't override their free will, so we're not really killers." She beamed.

"Technically," Dom said. "She was a threat, not just to you, but all the girls. She was getting worse but had isolated herself from the consequences of her actions. She would not have stopped."

"Was it the altar in the cabinet?" I asked, and Dom looked at me weird.

"What?" was all he said, Colleen inhaled through her teeth, and shook her head no.

"Colleen found a bunch of stuff in one of the cabinets that looked like some sort of altar to her." He was looking at me like I was nuts, Colleen had her head down and was focusing on aggressively petting Richard, who was purring loudly. "We thought at one point that Angel had killed Taylor and was running a death cult."

"What?" Dom said again. "Death cult? Where would you get such an idea?"

"Colleen found this death cult podcast called Dark Angel and when Taylor went missing, we thought it was her running it. The people at the club acted so weird around her. And there was an altar in the office cabinet. I swear it all made sense." But it didn't make any sense when I said it out loud. Like not at all. Colleen continued to pet Richard, and he continued to purr.

"That's ridiculous," he said, and his eyes landed on the pamphlet that Detective Shelton had left. He picked it up, "Colleen, I really think you need to take a look at this." She looked at him humbly.

"I may have gone down a rabbit hole there. After the pigeons killed Angel, I saw the manager throw away all that stuff in the cabinet. But there were like ashes and bones and stuff. And the podcaster really sounded like her, I swear." We both rolled our eyes at her, but she looked so sad.

"It's ok. Mistakes happen, and lots of smart people fall down internet rabbit holes. You were so much help at the club though. Saved me from a boring office job, or even worse. Retail." I smiled at her, but her look didn't change.

"About that…." She said. "I thought I was helping to influence those guys, but it was all you. I can't influence people. Just seduce them."

"Huh, I guess I can't really be mad at that." And I wasn't. That confidence I thought I was faking turned out to be justified. So good for me.

"No, because you're beautiful. And I love you!" She dumped Richard off her lap and jumped on top of me in an aggressive embrace. It was like being attacked by an overzealous Labrador. Except in a pink bunny suit and way sexier.

When her grip let up, I said to Dom, "So she can live just fine without killing anyone? Like forever?"

"I don't know about forever. But yes. Succubae and Incubi can get what they need without killing. She could, or I could," he gave me a Colleen-esqe look from under his dark lashes that made me short of breath, "We only need one human in fact. She doesn't even need to visit other people."

Colleen looked surprised, "Wait what? But that insatiable need, that craving I feel must mean I need that."

"That's just a feeling, a strong one, but that's all it is." Dom said. "Lacey is enough…for both of us." Oh my god, was he asking me to go steady?

"Ok!" Colleen said, "Just Lacey."

"We can each feed off each other too," Dom said to Colleen, and she brightened.

"So, no more death?" I asked.

"Nope." Dom said.

"I guess that about settles it then." I said, it didn't really though. I'm sure there were a ton of other things I probably needed to know. But the two most important things were clear. There would be no more death, and Colleen and Dom seemed like they were going to get along.

No more cops, no more Angel, plus I had proved that I could resist them if I wanted. And I was all done resisting.

"Perfect. Hey, Dom, would you like to see our bedroom?" I tried that wink, and I don't know if I nailed it or not, but Dom was up and on his feet before the question was even out of my mouth. Naked again, he picked me up in his arms and carried me into the bedroom. Colleen bounded behind us still in her bunny suit. But it disappeared as she went through the doorway.

34

Colleen

Maybe Dom's not so bad. Actually, he's fucking amazing. Like on all the levels. We dropped our wings as we hit the bed with Lacey. They just got in the way. Lips and nipples and demon cock, it wasn't anything like sex with dreaming humans. I was afraid we might accidently fuck poor Lacey to death. But our Lacey, she's a trooper. Yes, I said *our*. She's ours now. But only because she wants to be. We're a happy threesome.

In a convenient turn of events, the Embers Gentleman's Club needed a new door girl. I know, right? And who just happened to have a glowing recommendation from their favorite bouncer and the social security number of a dead lady named Kayla in Kansas? Me! I offered to do the bookkeeping too. I don't know anything about it, but I told Dom that I was sure I could find a video or two and learn how. He said that wasn't a good idea.

I don't think Dom or Lacey appreciate my research skills. But I'm much more careful now. I stay away from conspiracy videos. I only look at real stuff now. Like how the earth is really flat.

I'm learning to cook, actually. And I'm getting pretty good. I've tried a ton of new recipes and new foods. There are way better things than pizza with pineapple it turns out. I just make sure to avoid anything with chemicals or GMOs. Did you know that GMOs were invented for population control? And yeah, I know all that stuff isn't true, but it's fascinating the shit that people will make up for a buck. And how easy it can be for even smart people to be misled.

I had been searching for something. My identity, my place in the world or just in Lacey's world. I thought I had been looking and finding answers, but what I found were just guesses. Myths and stories that filled the enormous gaps in my knowledge. I remember nothing from before I came to Lacey. All I had were gaps. And I did my best to fill them. It's just that I filled those gaps with a bunch of bullshit. Finding Dom filled some of those gaps for real. In a few different ways. I know that I am a bi-sexual succubus in a polyamorous relationship with a human. I had been desperately searching for a label. A box to fit in, and now that I have them, they seem totally unimportant. I found love. What the fuck else is there?

Not that Dom knows everything. But he says that learning is all a part of the journey we're on. He is so fucking smart. He knows the nothingness that I did before he came to his first love. And he was fortunate to learn from her as much as he could. He will be my guide as we bumble fuck our way through whatever this existence is. We don't know what came before we existed, and we don't know what will come after. All we know is that we have this moment right now. This moment. This life. And we have Lacey, and so much to learn about the world. So maybe it's better to not have all the answers. It's hard to be comfortable with not knowing, but it's much easier when you have people to figure it out with you.

About the Author

Erin Louis is a former adult entertainer with three non-fiction books about her life as a stripper as well as several short fiction stories.

She has a lifelong love of horror and dark humor.

Please check out her website at https://www.erinlouis.com/

OTHER HELLBOUND BOOKS

Stripper Noir

"I'm pretty much out of my "detective phase" now that I've finished Random, but I wanted to check it out. It's a nice detective murder thing with a twist and a very nice look at Vegas and the strip club scene. It's very accurate (as far as I know) strip club description and you never see that in a book, so that was nice. And a nice view of Vegas one doesn't usually get. I really enjoyed it." - Penn Jillette

Exotic Dancers are dying at an alarming rate in Las Vegas.

Former LVPD detective, Frank Michi, is roped into helping not only his former partner, but also the New Jersey mobsters who run the strip club, to unmask the psychopath who is running amok killing the dancers.

Can he figure it out in time - before more girls are brutally murdered?

South of Heaven

"Erin Louis's South of Heaven is a cutting critique of the very idea of Heaven and the paradoxes of paradise, wrapped in a delightfully irreverent tale. Godless cat-lovers will find it as relatable as those who ponder moral questions instead of taking their dictates from people claiming to speak for deities. "
- Andrew L. Seidel author of *American Crusade: How the Supreme Court Is Weaponizing Religious Freedom*

Kat, a lapsed Catholic and promiscuous stripper, never thought she would get into Heaven.

Even as she stands there at the Pearly Gates, she naturally expects to be sent directly to Hell. She picks a fight with St. Peter just for fun, but rules are rules, and Kat makes it into Heaven on a minor technicality.

Once there, Kat discovers, much to her dismay, the angels are jerks, the only music is God-awful Christian rock, and her brand-new halo comes with some most troubling conditions.

As if things weren't dismaying enough, Kay reunites with her father, who found eternal peace in a bottomless bottle of scotch, and her pot-smoking aunt, whose demon dealer resides in Hell. When she tracks down the demon, he tells Kat about his home in the desolate, fiery pit - where it rains blood but possesses all the earthly pleasures she misses so much in her disappointing afterlife.

Heaven isn't the paradise Kat was promised in Sunday school, and she wants out.

But will they let her go?

Flanagan

"Straw Dogs meets Fifty Shades - heart pounding, gut-wrenching, sexy as all hell and with a twist you'll never see coming!"

Meet the Sewells, your typical, all-American couple; happily married for ten years, respected high school teachers, still crazy about one another and with a secret, shared dark side.

During their annual Spring Break vacation to recharge their batteries and reconnect as a couple, they are waylaid by a perverse gang of misfits in the one horse, North Texas town of Flanagan.

Taken hostage as the focus of the gang's twisted games, the Sewells are brutalized into performing increasingly vicious physical, sexual and emotional acts upon one another, until events take an unexpected turn - triggered by an unintentional death.

As their circumstance descends into the worse nightmare imaginable, the Sewells find themselves involved in an altogether different situation...

The Gentleman's Choice

"A clever twist on the age old adage, Art imitates reality, drives this terrifying possibility into the deepest places of your imagination." Andrew Neiderman, author of *The Devil's Advocate* and the V.C. Andrews novels.

A sleazy internet dating show blamed for a viewer's death, a host with a dark, secret past, and a killer with a sadistic grudge…

Someone is kidnapping and murdering previous contestants from the popular streaming show *The Gentleman's Choice* – a strictly adult hybrid of *The Bachelor and Love Island.* Private Investigator, Vanessa Young, is hired by a victim's family to infiltrate the show as a contestant to expose and capture the killer.

Vanessa and Cole Gianni, the show's charismatic star, begin to fall romantically for each other, until Vanessa's plan goes terribly awry when they're drugged and taken to a remote location to take part in their captor's own brutal, ultimately fatal, version of *The Gentleman's Choice*. With the clock ticking toward their fateful final night, Vanessa and Cole are forced into a battle of wills to survive their tormentor and escape with their lives before it's too late…

**A HellBound Books LLC
Publication**

www.hellboundbookspublishing.com